C0-ASN-366

A SOUTHERN AFRICAN
READ ALOUD BOOK
COMPILED BY JAY HEALE
ILLUSTRATED BY ALIDA BOTHMA

TAFELBERG

"The little hare" by Jay Heale first appeared in *The Pink Fairy Book* (Kestrel Books, London, 1982); "An aloe story" by Madeline Murgatroyd first appeared in *Tales from the Kraals* (Howard Timmins, Cape Town, 1968 and 1981).

28 Wale Street, Cape Town

Design and typography by Linda Rademeyer
Cover illustration by Alida Bothma
Set in 12 on 14 pt Palacio by Diatype Setting
Lithographic reproduction by Unifoto, Cape Town
Printed by National Book Printers, Goodwood, Cape
First edition 1987

ISBN 0 624 02005 3

Contents

The art of reading aloud

"Story time" is a moment of magic. No recorded programme on television or video can ever replace the warmth of a story told at mother's knee or the dreaming adventure of a bedtime tale. It is a time of physical as well as mental contact with your child, as you share the pages together. Listening to stories, your child develops imagination, and starts to appreciate basic moral values.

In the process of reading aloud, you are not setting out to teach your child to read, you are teaching your child to *want* to read. That is more important, and it must come first. Reading is enjoyment – not a subject at school.

Storytelling is as old as Africa, and all the stories in this book have their setting in Southern Africa. They can instruct, warn, intrigue, excite or delight the hearer. But we must ensure always that the teller of tales and the audience enjoy the process equally.

HOW TO USE THIS BOOK

It is best always to read the story through to yourself beforehand. That way you know the "shape" of the story and you can relax or quicken the pace as the story demands. Use different voices for the various characters if you can, too. If you spot a word too difficult for your child to understand, don't be afraid to put a synonym in its place. But don't stop and explain words: children can understand what's happening in a story even if individual words pass them by. For most children, new words are a fascination.

Allow yourselves the pleasure of imagining round the story when it is finished. Discuss the reactions of the characters. Did it end the way it should? What would we have done if we had been there? That helps a child to identify, and so turn the printed word into reality.

A child who asks to hear a certain story, over and over again, is merely calling for the repetition of a pleasurable process – like the need for another cigarette or today's sundowner! It is also no small compliment to the author. Repetition breeds a feeling of security.

This collection of stories and poems is intended for children between the ages of about four and eight. It is arranged approximately in order of difficulty, with the easiest stories first. Though the many authors were encouraged to write in their own styles, the common link between all these stories is their relevance to South African children today. Here are the landscapes, the animals and characters of the world they live in.

Children enjoy finding out. They like to know more than we might suppose. The "DID YOU KNOW?" boxes are not really intended as part of the Read Aloud process – they are snippets of information which you can add for extra benefit when the moment seems right. Information and imagination can be advantageously blended.

AS THEY GROW

Although these stories and poems have been chosen for listeners too young to read to themselves, do not stop reading aloud just because your child has learnt to read alone. His need for stories remains just as great, and your own reading encourages the process and sets the seal of approval. Reading is not merely something done at school. That is a most vital point to establish.

By using this book – and others – you will have created the enjoyment of reading, the fun of books. Your child will have learnt that stories are fun, and that there are good stories about his own country. You will have shared a warm moment of communication which no video, microchip or machine can ever supply. Congratulations – and happy reading!

Jay Heale

Jay Heale

A South African alphabet

A is for ***A**loe* **a**lone at **A**i-**A**is
alongside an **a**ardvark **a**fraid of the mice.

B is for ***B**ishop-**B**ird*, **b**right red and **b**lack,
boarding the **B**lue Train past **B**ellville and **b**ack.

C is the ***C**oelacanth* **c**aught 'neath the waves
considered extinct as the **C**ape **C**ango **C**aves.

D is a ***D**assie* **d**elving **d**eep in a **d**onga,
digging for **d**iamonds – would he were stronger!

E is the ***E**agle* **e**ncircled in haze,
watching the **e**land and **e**lephant graze.

F for ***F**lamingo* where vlei water's **f**lowing,
flapping pink wings beside **f**reesia **f**lowers growing.

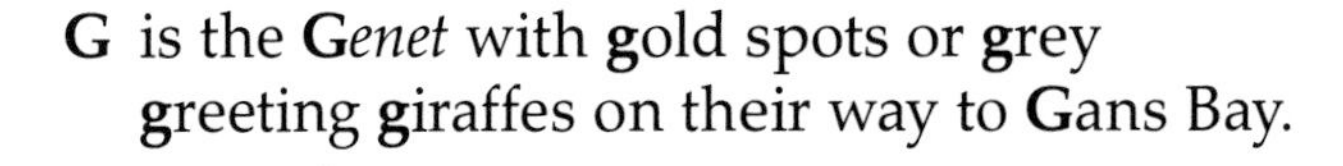

G is the ***G**enet* with **g**old spots or **g**rey
greeting **g**iraffes on their way to **G**ans Bay.

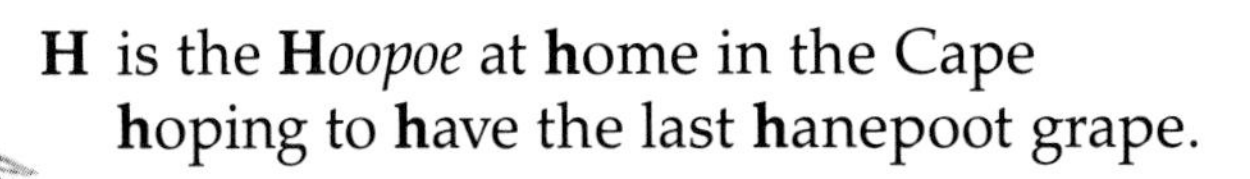

H is the ***H**oopoe* at **h**ome in the Cape
hoping to **h**ave the last **h**anepoot grape.

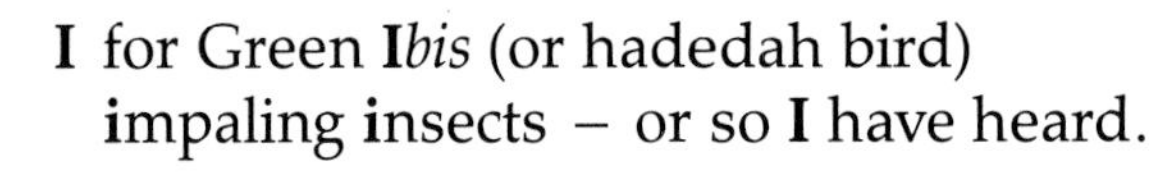

I for Green ***I**bis* (or hadedah bird)
impaling **i**nsects – or so **I** have heard.

J is the ***J**ackal* beneath **j**acaranda
enjoying a **j**og on your stoep (or verandah).

K is the ***K**lipspringer* in the **K**aroo –
climbing the **k**oppies of the **K**ruger Park too.

L is the ***L**ion* Doctor **L**ivingstone found
close to his **l**aager where **l**ocusts abound.

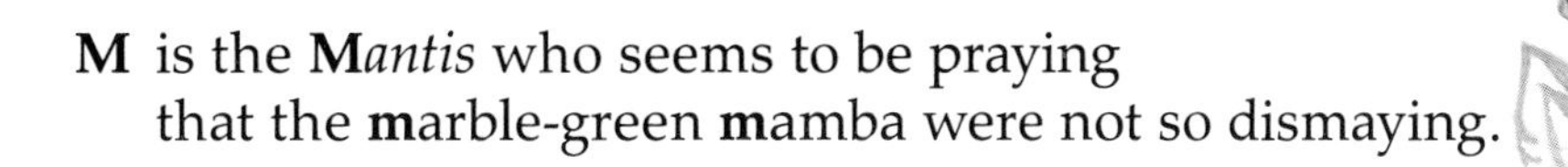

M is the *__M__antis* who seems to be praying
that the **m**arble-green **m**amba were not so dismaying.

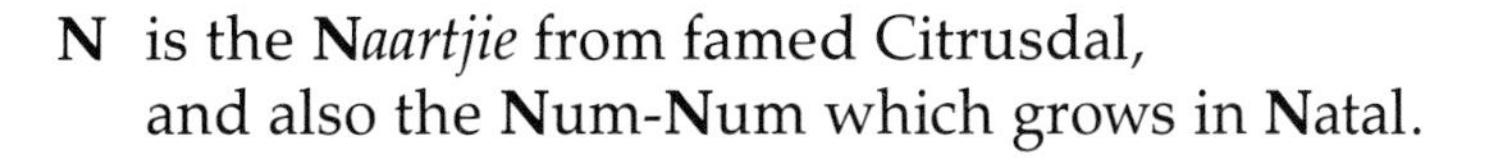

N is the *__N__aartjie* from famed Citrusdal,
and also the **N**um-**N**um which grows in **N**atal.

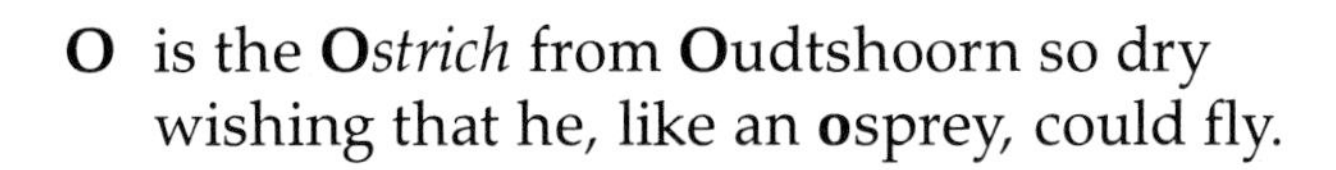

O is the *__O__strich* from **O**udtshoorn so dry
wishing that he, like an **o**sprey, could fly.

P is a *__P__elican* **p**lunging at "**P**lett"
from his **p**erch on a **p**epper-tree in silhouette.

Q was the *__Q__uagga*, a zebra-striped horse,
the **q**uarry of hunters who showed no remorse.

R is a *__R__hino*, in the **r**ed, **r**usty sand,
running a **r**ace to the Witwaters**r**and.

S is the *__S__hark* in our **s**outherly **s**ea,
proud of his picture on **S**.A.T.V.

T is the stone that we call *__T__iger's eye* –
found in the **T**ransvaal and not in **T**ranskei.

U for an *__U__mfaan* who's **u**rging an ox
on his way from **U**mtata to **U**mhlanga Rocks.

V is the *__V__oortrekker* over the **V**aal
shooting at **v**ultures and talking the "taal".

W – *__W__eaver-birds*, stealing the corn,
weaving their nests in a **W**ait-a-bit thorn.

X is a *__X__hosa* (the click's hard to say!)
playing a **x**ylophone quite his own way.

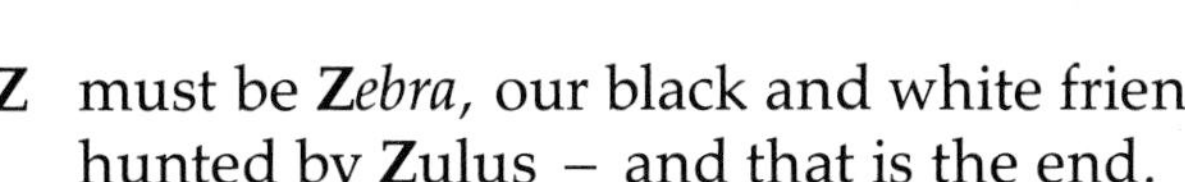

Y is the *__Y__ellowwood*, free from all knots,
used to make furniture, flooring and **y**achts.

Z must be *__Z__ebra*, our black and white friend,
hunted by **Z**ulus – and that is the end.

Barbara Rowland

The little tree

There was once a little marula tree growing in the tough dry grass. Its stem was thin and it had only a few dark leaves.

One day Elephant came by. The little tree rustled its leaves. "Please don't tread on me," it whispered.

Elephant stopped. "Why mustn't I tread on you?" he asked.

"Because you are huge and I am small! If you crush me, I can't grow up and help people."

"Oh!" said Elephant. "A little twig like you? Who do you think you could help? Could you help me?"

"Yes," said the little tree firmly.

"Will you help birds like hornbills, owls and weavers?"

"Yes," said the little tree.

"And will you help animals like warthogs, baboons and giraffes?"

"I will help them all when I am big," said the little tree. "Just let me grow."

"All right," said Elephant, who was kind although he was clumsy with his feet. "I won't tread on you. When you are big I shall come back and see how much you can really help."

The sun shone on little Marula Tree, the

rain fell on it, and the years went by. All the time it grew until it was a great spreading tree.

One day Elephant wandered along. He was older too, and his cracked grey skin had many extra folds and wrinkles. It was hot, and he stood in the cool shade of the marula tree. He waved his great ears backwards and forwards.

"Yes," said Elephant, "I remember you, Marula Tree. You have grown big enough to shade even someone like me. You are helping me, as you said you would – helping me to stay cool."

"The kudu and the zebra also rest in my shade," said the tree. "Baboons squabble with each other for my creamy fruit. You enjoy it too, Elephant. And the warthogs crack the kernels to eat them."

"What about the birds you said you would help?" asked Elephant.

"Look up," said the tree.

Elephant looked. Sitting on a pale grey branch was an owl.

"Owl sleeps in my branches in the daytime," said the tree.

The owl opened one yellow eye and stared at Elephant. Then he closed his eye and went to sleep again.

"Did you see those nests hanging from my branches? Those are weavers' nests. I told you I would help the weavers."

"What about the hornbills, and the giraffe?" asked Elephant.

"In front of you is a hole in my bark. Sticking out is Mother Hornbill's beak. She is inside there sitting on her eggs."

Just then Giraffe came walking towards them. "Do you mind if I eat some of your juicy leaves, Marula Tree?" he said. "I am hungry."

"Eat them," replied the tree. "I have plenty."

"You are right," said Elephant to the marula tree. "You do help people. I am glad I didn't tread on you when you were small."

DID YOU KNOW?

The *marula* is one of the most important trees for men and animals. Elephant, giraffe, zebra, rhino and kudu browse on the green leaves, while smaller buck and porcupines chew at the roots and the dry leaves. The marula tree produces masses of cream-coloured fruit about the size of a plum. Many animals enjoy eating these, especially baboons. Human beings also gather the marula fruit and make beer from it. The kernels from the stone inside the fruit make valuable food, as they are rich in protein and vitamin C. Men and animals are grateful to the marula tree for the cool shade under its thick spreading branches, but unfortunately mosquitoes like it too, and they breed in the moist holes in the bark. The wood is soft and is used for carving bowls and dishes. Because of its many uses, some Africans regard the marula as a magic tree.

Jenny Seed

The china egg

"Well, I am disappointed in you," said Jill, looking in dismay at the empty laying nest in the fowl house. She had brought a little basket down from the kitchen to collect the eggs. "No eggs again! You are three naughty hens! You haven't laid any eggs for two weeks."

Poppy, the biggest of the three New Hampshire hens, stopped scratching for mealies in the dry grass and said, "Cawk, cawk, cawk!"

Specky, the plump, fluffy-tailed one, stopped digging herself into her sand bath and said, "Cluk, cluk, cluk!"

Goldie, the dignified golden brown one, stopped pecking at the mash in the feed trough and said, "Bak, bak, bakkeek!"

"It's no use clucking and cawking like that," said Jill sternly. "You've got to do something. It's my birthday on Saturday and if you don't lay any eggs how can Mummy make me a cake?"

She shook her head at the three hens. "Please, Poppy, Specky and Goldie," she said. "Please lay me some lovely brown eggs tomorrow."

The hens cocked their heads and stared up at her with sharp black eyes. They looked very indignant. If they could have spoken they might have said, "You don't understand at all, Jill. You think that we aren't laying any eggs, but we are. We lay eggs every day!"

But they could not talk and so they could not explain to Jill that it was the big leguan that lived in the rocks behind the fowl run that had been coming every day for the last two weeks to steal their eggs. Early in the morning he would slither under the wire netting, flattening his long grey lizard-like body and flicking his quick forked tongue in and out in his eagerness for his breakfast.

"Kraak, kuk, kuk, kuk," was all the three New Hampshire hens could say very sadly. They had always been so proud of the big brown eggs they laid.

Just then Jill's mother came into the run. In her hand was something white and shiny.

"No eggs again today?" she asked. "Let's put this china egg into the laying nest. The hens may think it's a real egg and they may lay some of their own next to it. It's an old trick poultry-keepers sometimes use to get the hens to lay."

"Bak, bak, bak," said the hens disdainfully after Jill and her mother had gone. They examined the china egg and pecked at it cautiously. They did not think that the cold shiny white egg looked anything like their own lovely brown ones.

The next day the leguan was so eager to eat eggs that he came even earlier than usual into the run. He wriggled under the wire netting and scrambled on his short scaly legs into the hen house. The hens had not yet laid their eggs. Only the china egg lay in the nest.

"Cawk, cawk, cawk!" said Poppy.

"Cluk, cluk, cluk!" said Specky.

"Bak, bak, bakkeek!" said Goldie.

The leguan took no notice of the hens. He thrust his snake-like head into the laying

nest and in his haste swallowed the china egg. He stopped quite still in surprise. His eyes were wide and staring. His mouth opened, then closed, then opened again.

If the leguan could have spoken he might have said, "Haa! What sort of egg was that? It feels like a stone in my stomach! What trick did you hens play on me? Haa! What a nasty egg!"

The leguan made off as fast as he could under the wire and disappeared among the rocks.

"Kraak, kuk, kuk!" said the hens, staring after him.

Later that morning Jill came down with her basket to see if the china egg had encouraged the New Hampshires to lay. She laughed for joy when she saw the nest. "Three eggs!" she exclaimed. "What good hens you are! I shall have a lovely birthday cake after all."

Then she looked around in bewilderment. "But where's the china egg?" she asked. "That's odd. It's disappeared."

"Cluk, cluk, cluk!" said Specky.

"Cawk, cawk, cawk!" said Poppy.

"Bak, bak, bakkeek!" said Goldie.

Jill and her mother never did discover what had become of the china egg. Specky and Poppy and Goldie knew, of course, but they could not tell. And the leguan knew, but he never came back into the fowl run again, so he could not tell either.

DID YOU KNOW?

The *leguan* is the largest lizard in South Africa. You can find them right the way through Africa, in India, the East Indies and even in Australia.

There are two types of leguan in South Africa. The water leguan is slim, an expert swimmer that eats mostly mussels and crabs. The rock (or tree) leguan has a thicker body and is shorter – usually not more than a metre long. It climbs trees and rocks skilfully, and wanders all over the veld in search of food – for it will eat almost any living thing smaller than itself, and it is very fond of eggs. It is a bad-tempered creature, so be careful. The leguan will swell itself up and hiss at you, and lash out fiercely with its tough scaly tail.

Jennifer Forshaw

Cape Town birthday

Tomorrow's my birthday, and Daddy has said
that if I am specially good,
he'll take us out, my sister and me,
for a picnic in the wood.

Perhaps up to Rhodes Memorial
where the trees reach right to the sky,
and after our picnic we'll climb the hills,
my daddy, my sister and I.

Perhaps we'll go to the Gardens –
I once went there with my school –
and we'll wave our fingers gently
to the fish that swim in the pool.

Perhaps we'll go to Kirstenbosch
and follow the winding path
until we come to that shady spot
by Lady Anne Barnard's bath.

There are so many places to choose between
for our picnic in the wood.
I really can't wait for tomorrow,
and I'm trying so hard to be good.

Oonagh Pienaar

The jackal's breakfast

In the Nkandla forest of Zululand lived a silver-backed jackal. He was about as big as a medium-sized dog, with a sharp nose, and he was thin and always hungry.

One morning this particular jackal woke up feeling very hungry, so he crept behind a tree which stood beside the path that ran through the forest. He waited and waited for someone to come along the path – someone he could have for breakfast!

At last his sharp ears heard the pitter patter of little feet. The jackal jumped out from behind the tree right in front of a little mouse. The mouse stopped, too frightened to move.

"Good morning, Mrs Mouse!" barked the jackal, licking his lips at the same time.

"Good morning, Mr Jackal!" squeaked the mouse in a trembling sort of squeak.

"I'm hungry, Mrs Mouse," barked the jackal. "Won't you come and have breakfast with me?"

"No thank you, Mr Jackal," squeaked the mouse. "I have my hungry babies to find food for. But my friend the dassie will be coming this way soon, and he might like to have breakfast with you. He's much bigger and fatter than me. Now please let me past. I'm in a hurry to get back to my babies."

The jackal was very hungry, but he was also very greedy, and the thought of a nice plump dassie made his mouth water, so he moved aside and Mrs Mouse scurried off as fast as her little paws could go.

The jackal crept back behind the tree which stood beside the path that ran through the forest.

This time he did not have to wait for long. A fat furry dassie came hopping round the corner. The jackal jumped out from behind his tree right in front of the surprised dassie.

"Good morning, Master Dassie!" barked the jackal. "Nice day, isn't it? Would you like to come and have breakfast with me?" And he licked his lips in a hungry sort of way.

"Good morning, Mr Jackal – no thank you," stuttered the dassie quickly, looking at the jackal's sharp white teeth. "I've already had my breakfast, but my friend Mrs Guinea-fowl will be coming along in a minute. She might like to join you for breakfast. She's bigger than I am, and fatter too. Now please won't you let me past? I do want to join my mates on the rocks near the stream."

The greedy jackal thought about the nice plump guinea-fowl who would be coming along in a minute, so he moved out of the path and the dassie hopped on as quickly as he could.

Once again the jackal crept behind the tree which stood beside the path that ran through the forest. He was so hungry now that his tummy gave a groan.

At last a guinea-fowl came strutting down the path.

Out jumped the jackal.

The guinea-fowl stopped with a squawk and a flutter of her spotted wings.

"Good morning, Mrs Guinea-fowl!" barked the jackal, licking his lips at the same time. Here was just the breakfast he had been waiting for.

The guinea-fowl looked at the jackal with one beady eye, then she turned her head and looked at him with the other beady eye.

"Mrs Guinea-fowl, I'm so hungry. Won't you have breakfast with me?" barked the jackal, just longing to pounce on her.

"No thank you, Mr Jackal," cheeped the guinea-fowl. "I've already had my breakfast. My friend will be coming this way, though. I saw him a little way back. He's even bigger and fatter than I am, and I'm sure you would like to have him for breakfast. Now please let me past. I'm in a hurry to get back to my eggs."

The jackal was now so hungry that his tummy rumbled very loudly indeed, but he was still very greedy. The thought of a bigger and fatter breakfast made him move out of the path, and the guinea-fowl ran off quickly, calling loudly, the way guinea-fowls do when they are scared.

Once again the jackal crept behind the tree which stood beside the path that ran through the forest. It was getting hot now and he was feeling thirsty as well as very hungry. In fact, he was so hungry that it felt as if his ribs were knocking together.

At long last he heard a rustling noise. Someone was coming along the path! The jackal licked his lips again. This time he would have his breakfast, no matter what sort of animal it was. The rustling noise drew nearer and the jackal sprang out into the path and bumped right into a very large hairy bush pig with fierce-looking tusks sticking out on either side of his whiskery snout.

The bush pig stopped and glared at the skinny jackal. The spiky hair on his broad back rose and he snorted loudly.

"G-g-g-good m-m-morning, Mr Bush Pig," stammered the jackal, eyeing those fearsome tusks.

"Good morning yourself," snorted the bush pig very crossly. "How dare you jump out in front of me? Just move before I butt you with my tusks. I'm in a hurry to get to the vlei to dig for bulbs."

"C-c-c-certainly, M-m-mr B-b-bush Pig," yelped the jackal, as the bush pig rushed past him, just touching his skinny side with the tip of one tusk.

"Haven't you perhaps a friend following you? A smaller friend?" he called hopefully as the enormous bush pig blundered off. The bad-tempered bush pig snorted and disappeared down the path.

The greedy jackal stood in the path. His tail drooped between his legs and his tummy rumbled emptily.

"Ah well, no breakfast today," he whined to himself, and trotted back along the path that ran through the Nkandla forest.

DID YOU KNOW?

The most common *jackal* in South Africa is the black-backed jackal, which can be found in any type of countryside from the dry Namib desert across the open Karoo to the green valleys of Natal. It has become a great menace to the sheep farmers in the Karoo. But the more it is hunted with guns, poison and traps, the more cunning the jackal seems to become. Although it is mostly a carrion eater (living off the remains of dead animals), it also hunts for itself, and will eat insects, lizards, grapes, watermelons and pineapple – in fact, almost anything available!

The jackal normally hunts at night, and its high-pitched howl is well known to those who have lived (or camped) in the open veld.

Dora Tudor

The orange train

In Cape Town Station there are rows and rows of trains. All the trains have brown roofs and brown sides with grey round the windows and grey on the doors. They are all very dull. And when they get dusty and dirty they are duller than ever.

One of these dull brown and grey trains went to the yard to be repainted because the brown and grey paint was peeling badly. At the yard the painters scraped off all the brown and grey paint. Then they gave the train a waterproof undercoat of lovely bright orange paint.

The orange was so bright and so lovely that all the other trains looked round to see where the bright orange colour was coming from. The orange train looked down at his front, along his sides and up to his roof. Everywhere was a lovely bright orange colour and he wriggled inside with happiness. All night long while the paint dried he thought, "I like being orange. I like being bright orange. I am going to stay bright orange for ever and ever."

The moon looked down and smiled and lit up his orange roof. The stars twinkled on his orange sides and the wind blew gently round the orange doors. By morning he was quite dry.

When the sun came up two painters arrived to finish painting the orange train. One had a brush and a tin of grey paint and the other had a brush and a tin of brown paint. "We must finish this train today," they said.

"No! no! no!" said the orange train. "I love being orange. I am going to stay orange forever. Please don't paint me brown and grey again."

But the painters opened their tins of paint and dipped their brushes into the brown and into the grey paint.

The orange train thought very quickly. He called to his driver to turn him on and before a spot of brown or grey paint splashed onto him he was driven backwards far away from the painters.

"Ha, ha," he thought. "They can't catch me now."

He rode backwards until he passed the Castle – the big stone fort built by the early settlers at the Cape. After the Castle he came to Cape Town Station. There he stopped because the line does not go any further. The station was full of school children waiting to catch their trains to school.

"Oh! Look at this train," shouted one little girl with a blazer and plaits, "it's orange. I'm going to catch the orange train."

"So am I, so am I," shouted the other children.

They all jumped on the orange train and laughed and swung their cases. The orange train took them to Observatory and to Mowbray and to Rondebosch and to Newlands where their schools were. They waved goodbye to him and ran off to tell their teachers about the orange train.

Then the orange train wanted to see the sea. At Muizenberg the beach comes right up to the railway line and the station. So the orange train set off for Muizenberg. At Claremont the bus drivers waved to him from the bridge and at Kenilworth an old lady with a walking stick stopped him.

"Please take me to Wynberg to draw my pension. You are the first train I can see properly," she said.

After that he had to stop at every station because everybody wanted to ride on the orange train.

This happened every day after that. Early in the morning the milkmen and the newspaper boys jumped into him. Then the delivery boys and the gardeners and the typists and the office workers all pushed into him. Later in the morning the shoppers carried their parcels into him and the little children ran up and down inside him.

So many people caught the orange train that his sides began to bulge and his wheels began to buckle. Some of his doors got jammed and once, when he was far too full, a window cracked and broke. He was getting worn out.

"What shall we do?" asked the mechanics who mend trains.

"What shall we do?" asked the conductors.

"What shall we do?" asked the ladies who clip tickets at the gate. "Everybody wants to ride on the orange train."

"He must be painted grey and brown like every other train," said the old engine who lives on the station.

"No!" said all the other trains. "We want to be painted orange . . . lovely bright happy orange . . . we want to be orange as well."

"No, you can't be orange," said the painters. "We haven't enough orange paint."

"No, you can't all be orange," said the mechanics. "You will look like a circus that carries elephants around."

"No, you can't all be orange," said the station master. "People will think we're a fun fair and not a proper railway."

"No, you can't . . . you can't . . . you can't," said everybody – even the head of the South African Railways.

So that is why all the trains at Cape Town Station are still brown and grey. And that is why they look a little dull and a little unhappy.

But if you are very lucky and look very carefully, you may catch a glimpse of the orange train. He is standing in the train yard near Woodstock Station waiting to be mended and he is still bright happy glowing orange.

DID YOU KNOW?

The *Blue Train* is South Africa's most famous train, travelling regularly from Pretoria to Cape Town. It was officially named "The Blue Train" in 1946, but the luxury train with its blue-painted coaches had been operating since 1927. Hot and cold water in your own compartment was a dream in those days, but the Blue Train had it. Nowadays, the compartments, lounge and dining-cars provide the equivalent of a top-class hotel, forever on the move – and moving at about 112 kilometres an hour!

C E Birkill

Plucking geese

Susie sat watching her mother pluck the goose. There were about fifty geese on the farm. She loved watching them having a swim in the dam. They made such a pretty picture as they waddled along with the sun shining on their wet white bodies. When the grass was at its greenest from the rains, that was the time of year for Mother to pluck the geese to get down for cushions.

"How sore it must be to have the downy feathers pulled off your breast," thought Susie. She looked at her mother holding a goose with her left hand, and with even strokes pulling off the down with her right hand.

"Mother, aren't you sorry for the poor goose? It must hurt her terribly," said Susie.

Mother collected together the down that she had plucked and thrown into the box next to her. She looked at Susie with a smile.

"You know, Susie, plucking does not really hurt the geese. It is too hot in summer to have so much down on your body. So I actually help them to feel cool and comfortable. Now, do you know what I'm going to do with this lovely soft down? I shall make a soft warm covering for Granny to use on cold winter nights. Don't you think that is a good idea?"

Susie curled up on her wooden stool and shivered. She knew that night time on their Karoo farm could be very chilly, and in the winter there was always frost and sometimes even snow. She nodded her head.

"Long ago," said Mother, "these coverings were called eiderdowns. They were stitched through to form pretty patterns, and filled with down from the eider duck. People today call them duvets. They are far lighter than blankets and just as warm. Granny will be pleased to be warm under her new duvet, and the geese will be pleased to feel cool."

Dora Tudor

The fern

In a house in Mowbray there lived a man and his wife called Uncle Lyndon and Auntie Elizabeth. They lived in a neat house with a blue fence and a blue gate. Little Mark Chapman could see their house quite plainly from where he lived. But he couldn't see what was happening inside!

One day Auntie Elizabeth brought home a little fern in a pot. She put it near to the window and gave it water to drink.

When Uncle Lyndon came home he looked at the fern.

"This is a pretty little fern," he said and he also gave it water to drink.

After that Auntie Elizabeth looked at the fern every day and dusted carefully around it and watered it.

When Uncle Lyndon came home from work he went to look at the fern.

"It looks so pretty," he always said, "and see how well it is growing."

After a few weeks Uncle Lyndon said to Auntie Elizabeth, "Our fern is growing very well. You must move the dining-room table, otherwise we shall brush against it."

So Auntie Elizabeth moved the dining-room table.

After several more weeks Auntie Elizabeth had a dinner party. The fern reached right over the guests' shoulders and tickled their ears and noses.

Auntie Elizabeth had to move the dinner table out of the dining-room and put it in the spare room at the back of the house.

Now when Uncle Lyndon came home he took a bucket of water to the fern. Sometimes he got lost among the branches. Then Auntie Elizabeth had to explore and find him.

After three more months Uncle Lyndon and Auntie Elizabeth had to move into the spare room at the back of the house with the dining-room table. The rest of the house was filling with waving green fronds.

At the end of the year the fern was peeping out of the chimney and bulging through the windows. It looked beautiful and everybody stopped in the road to admire it. All except little Mark Chapman, who got nervous and stayed indoors for a week.

"This is too much," said Uncle Lyndon one morning. "My back is stiff and sore from sleeping on the spare room floor. *The fern must go!"*

Auntie Elizabeth cried a little. Then she said in a very small voice, "Yes, dear. The fern must go."

They hired a tractor to pull the fern out of the front door.

"Let us give the fern to the church," they said. "It will look beautiful in the church."

The tractor pulled the fern to the church on a trailer. The fern did indeed look very beautiful in the church.

BUT . . .
the congregation
could not see the minister,
the minister could not see the clock,
Uncle Lyndon could not find the organ,
and little Mark Chapman got lost.

So the minister announced, "Beloved brethren, this fern must go."

The beloved brethren (but not the beloved sisters, because they keep silent in church) called out "Where to?" from under the fern.

Everybody thought and thought.

At last somebody found Mark Chapman, who said, "I thought I was at Kirstenbosch."

"Kirstenbosch. The very place," said the congregation. So they all helped to move the fern to Kirstenbosch Botanical Gardens, on the slopes of Table Mountain.

They planted it near to Lady Anne Barnard's bath, where there are lots of other ferns. Children played hide-and-seek in it and gardeners slept under it.

But Uncle Lyndon and Auntie Elizabeth were able to sleep comfortably in their own house once again.

After two years the people of Cape Town began to write letters to the newspapers. They wrote lots and lots of letters.

"This fern must go," they wrote. "We can't see Table Mountain!"

Little Mark Chapman suggested that they should move Table Mountain, but no one is quite sure what will happen next.

DID YOU KNOW?

Kirstenbosch is the mountainside home of the National Botanical Gardens of South Africa. The area was a gift from Cecil Rhodes to the people of this country. Since 1913 it has been a display garden of our own South African plants and about 4 000 different species grow there. If you can visit Kirstenbosch, make sure you see the many succulents growing in the rock garden, the ferny dell and the hundreds of different varieties of protea – our national flower. There's a spring flowing into what they call Lady Anne Barnard's bath, and people say that a coin dropped in will bring you luck. The gardens are open throughout the year from sunrise to sunset, and there is a tearoom which serves refreshments and lunches.

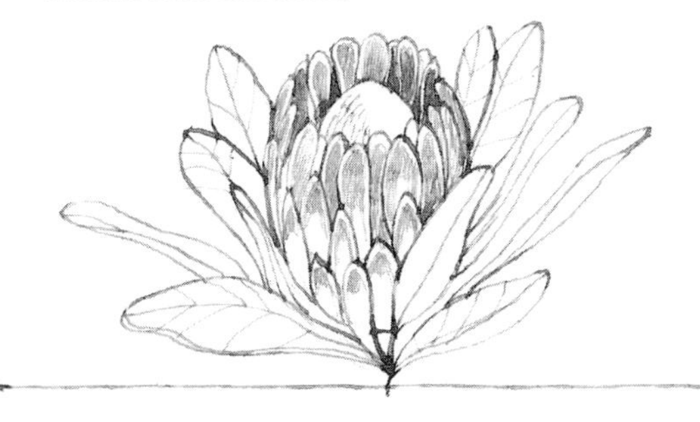

Yvonne Bremner

Jake

One day, we said that we would make
a lovely cake for little Jake,
but No! He wanted us to take
our fishing rods, and find a lake,
and catch a whopping great big hake,
then gather twigs up with a rake,
and make a fire to bake the hake.
He said, he didn't want a cake.

We said,
            that one could catch a hake
down at the sea, not in a lake.
His little fists began to shake.
"Then go to the sea and catch a hake,
and hurry up for goodness' sake."

We said,
            we could not catch a hake
without a boat in sea or lake,
and he would *have* to have a cake.
He yelled,
            "I do not want a cake,
I've told you all I want is hake."

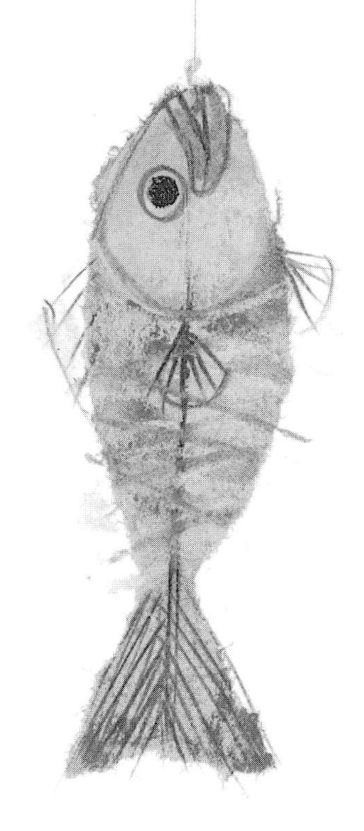

We thought and thought how we could make
the kind of cake that Jake would take.
Of course, we would buy frozen hake,
then mix in flour and eggs and bake
a golden, crispy, fishy cake.

Oh! happy boy, Oh! smiling Jake,
he ate too much of that fish cake,
and got a dreadful tummy ache.

Nora Cobbledick

Dreamflight

Themba lazily chewed the end of a long piece of grass as he lay looking up into the blue African sky. He was only six years old and very proud to be in charge of the family's herd although it could get very lonely with only the cattle and the goats for company.

As he lay watching the little white clouds chasing each other across the sky, he wished that he could join them in their games. Their fluffiness reminded him of the white goatskins that his father and the other men wore around their legs when they did their traditional dances, and he leapt up stamping his feet and pretending to be a brave Zulu warrior. Even brave Zulu warriors get tired, though, and little Themba only had short legs. So, with a final leap into the air, he fell down and rolled over and over until he was once again lying on his back, this time a little breathless.

In English his name means My Hope, and Themba's hope was that one day he would fly like the clouds he was watching right over the distant mountains and all the way to Durban, where his father worked in a big factory.

He had never seen a factory, but his father had told him that it was bigger than all the huts that his eyes could see joined together under one roof. There were big machines that made the tractor that belonged to their Chief look like a toy, and the noise that they made was like a hundred thunder-storms all shouting at once.

Hawu, he thought, my father is very brave to work in such a place.

A cool breeze began to tease him and Themba pulled his blanket more closely around his shoulders. He clutched his beaded stick with both hands and slowly let his heavy eyelids droop. He drifted off to sleep with his head full of dreams.

Suddenly he became aware that he was floating. He opened his eyes and looked around him. To his surprise he found that he was lying on one of the very clouds that he had been watching before he fell asleep.

He sat up and looked down. Far below him he could see his village.

The women were busy grinding mealies in front of the huts and some were washing their clothes in the stream. The little umfaans were playing their games, kicking up the dust as they ran barefoot between the huts. The dogs were lying sleeping in the shade and the smoke from the fires slowly drifted up towards him.

The kraals were left far behind as the wind blew his little cloud along. Soon he was flying over the tops of the high mountains that he had only seen before in the far distance. He sank down a little further into the soft woolly cloud in case he fell off, and peeped over the edge.

Far below him he saw a family of goats playing on the rocks. From his high perch they reminded him of mice and he laughed as he watched them jump from rock to rock. An eagle wheeled in the sky above him and screeched when he saw Themba peering up at him from the middle of a cloud.

Themba saw the little streams that started

high up in the mountains tumbling down over the rocks and then all joining together to become a large river that slowly found its way to the sea.

When the mountains were left behind he saw villages like the one he sometimes went to with his mother to buy the things they needed from the store. He did not go often because it was a full day's walk there and a full day's walk back – much too far for his short legs. Besides, he had to look after the cattle and feed the chickens while his mother was away.

The cattle in the fields below looked like little clay cows and the fields themselves looked like the squares of blanket his grandmother had made him out of different colours of wool.

Then he saw a sight which made him catch his breath. There were many big huts made of stone such as he had never seen before. Some of them had dams right outside and people were jumping in and out of them. Themba had never seen such dams in his life and never such sparkling blue water – water the colour of the sky, not brown and muddy like the streams and the dams at home. He did not see any cattle or goats, so he thought that although these people had much water they must be very poor indeed.

What he saw next made him blink his

eyes. There were huge huts climbing right up into the sky. Who would live in such places? How would they climb to the top? Where did all the mud come from to build such places? How brave the indunas must be to climb up so high to build these big huts. The sun glinted off shiny squares and reflected in Themba's eyes. Tractors with brightly coloured roofs crawled around these big huts and they made him think of the many beetles he found in the veld.

Then below him he saw the most wonderful thing. A dam so large that no matter how hard he strained his eyes, he could not see where it ended. It must surely be the biggest dam in Africa.

My mummy and granny would be so happy to live next to such a dam, he thought. They would not have far to walk, balancing the water in buckets on their heads, if our kraal were here in this place. Our cattle and goats would be happy too. They would not have to wander far in search of water if the rains forgot to come.

But why were there huts floating on the dam? He had never seen huts floating on water before. He stared wide-eyed. He must remember everything to tell his mother and grandmother when he got back home.

Everything was so strange that Themba began to be just a little bit frightened, and he lay back in the softness of the little cloud and closed his eyes.

With a start he awoke. The ground was hard beneath him and the air was becoming cold.

Themba slowly sat up, rubbing the dust of his dreams from his eyes. He looked around him.

Below him on the slope the cattle and goats were still grazing, but further away now – slowly making their way back to the kraal. The sun was much lower in the sky, ready to slide down behind the mountains. He could see his friends in the distance, moving homewards behind their herds.

It was time for him to go home too – time for the milking. He stood up and stretched himself, his mind filled with all the wonderful things that he had seen.

When all his chores were done, Themba sat at the fireside with his mother and grandmother and his little sister Anna. His mother had cooked putu and made a stew with the dried beans his father had sent from the city and the meat of a rabbit that he, Themba, had caught the day before. Themba was hungry and he ate quickly, his fingers flying between his clay bowl and his mouth.

When the meal was finished, Themba drank a bowl of amaheu, the drink made of sour milk, which his grandmother had made, and leant back against the wall of the hut. His tummy was full and he was content. His little sister was asleep on their mother's back and he watched her head roll slightly as their mother moved around clearing away the remains of the meal. In the distance a dog barked and close by was the comforting sound of the cattle moving around.

Themba moved closer to the fire and began to tell his mother of his wonderful adventure – about how he had floated on a cloud and all the strange things he had seen. She laughed gently and told him that he had been dreaming and the things he had seen were all remembered stories he had heard from his father.

It was time for him to sleep now, she said. He had to get up with the rooster in time to milk the two cows before he went back up to the hills with the herd.

Themba went into the hut and rolled himself up in his blankets. As he lay in the darkness he wondered if what his mother had said was true – that he had been dreaming. But no – he was sure that he had been sitting on that little cloud floating through the sky like a feather drifting in the wind.

Jay Heale

Plenty of room!

A very long time ago, when even old Africa was very young, everybody lived together. They had their own little houses, of course, but they all lived on the earth side by side. Man lived there, and Lion and Elephant and Mantis and Locust, and so did Sun and Moon. That's what this story is all about.

It may sound strange, but it's only just started. You wait!

Now, Sun was Moon's husband and Moon was Sun's wife, and one of their best friends was Water. They liked visiting all sorts of people, but they liked visiting Water best of all. He was an exciting sort of person to visit – deep and mysterious, with all the fishes and seaweeds and whales and barnacles.

One day when Sun was out visiting, smiling warmly at all of his friends, he began to wonder why none of them ever came to visit him.

"Water, my dear friend," said Sun, "why don't you come and pay *me* a visit one day? It's always my dear Moon and I who come visiting you."

"I'm afraid that your house just isn't big enough for me," said Water. "There are so many creatures I would have to bring with me. I couldn't leave them behind."

"Quite right!" said Sun. "You are as fond of your friends as I am. But I must have you come to visit me. I'll build a bigger house, that's what I'll do!"

So Sun hurried home and explained everything to Moon, and soon their old home had disappeared in a tumbling cloud of dust and you couldn't see the place for builders. Hundreds of them! Beams, walls, thatching – all of the very best, and the very biggest. Elephant poked his head in, shivered, and said it looked too huge and draughty for him. So he lumbered away.

"What a splendid new house!" said Sun and Moon when it was finished. "It's larger than any house there's ever been. Now we can invite all our friends, and Water must be the first."

Down to Water went Sun, beaming with delight. "Our house is ready!" he said proudly. "You must come and visit us at once. How about tomorrow?"

"I don't think it's a good idea," answered Water, rippling sadly to himself. "Who knows what might happen?"

"Nonsense, my dear friend. Nothing will go wrong," urged Sun. "We'll expect you in time for lunch." And home he went to help Moon prepare the party. In a big house it was going to be a very big party!

So, next morning, Water arrived at Sun's house with a gentle slapping, lapping sound. He poured himself in carefully until he covered all the floor, nearly a metre deep. No one could sit on the chairs any more, and all the rugs and carpets had floated away.

"I think I'd better stop like this," said Water.

"Don't be silly!" said Sun with some heat. "Look how much of you is left outside. What sort of a host would I be if I left most of my guests outside the door? Come in. There's plenty of room!"

So Water flowed in some more, and now he was two metres deep. Lobsters and squids were finishing up what was left of lunch, and coral was growing prettily on the window-sill.

"I'd better not come in any more," said Water.

"What are you going on about?" asked Sun, from where he stood on top of a cupboard. "There's plenty of room!"

"You really are welcome," said Moon shyly. "Do come in!"

So Water poured in even more. A shark scratched its itchy back on a table leg, seaweeds made green-brown patterns over the floor, and flying fish had games in and out of the rafters. Waves lapped right up to the ceiling, and Sun and Moon climbed outside on to the roof to escape being drowned. There was only a small triangle of air just under the very tip top of the roof.

Water was very worried to see his friends forced to sit up on the roof top. "I'm not meant to go visiting," he said. "You shouldn't have invited me in."

"Didn't I tell you we had a big house?" demanded Sun. "We built it specially. There's plenty of room. I insist that you come inside."

So Water gave a wet, sucking, smothering sigh and let himself pour in – all of him, every last sparkling drop. The waves rose and rose and covered the house, large as it was, right over the very top. Sun and Moon had no choice but to escape up into the sky.

And that, so they say, is why the Sun and Moon live so very far away and have never come down to earth again.

Madeline Murgatroyd

An aloe story

Many, many years ago there were no others but the black people living in this country. Among these there was one tribe more peaceful and hardworking than any other. They ploughed their lands, tended their mealies, fed their oxen and goats well and lived contented lives year after year.

Now, unfortunately, at this time, a fierce warlike tribe was also springing up. All the small clans round about had become filled with terror at the wicked doings of this impi that so often raided them. In order to keep the peace with them, the small clans had to agree helplessly to many of their demands.

One day Dombala, head of the peaceful tribe, received a message from the enemy chief which said, "Unless the best of your cattle and three loads of mealies are sent by tomorrow, I and my warriors will attack you and burn your huts."

"What?" cried Dombala. "Never will I bow my head to such a son of Satan. Return to your master," he said to the runner, "and tell him I and my people refuse to obey his command."

After the messenger had departed, Dombala sat thinking deeply for some time. Then he called his followers together and with tears in his eyes said, "Alas, my people, I am afraid I have brought great trouble on your heads. If you will give up your finest cattle and mealies, this cruel enemy may be contented. Do as you think best."

"No, no, O Chief!" cried all his warriors. "You answered as we wish. Let us fight this bully, and free our country once and for all."

"O, my people," answered the chief, "our numbers are few, but the strength of our hearts is great. Prepare then, for tomorrow before the sun rises beyond the hills, those demons will be here."

Then what excitement surged through the people! Young warriors sharpened their assegais; huge knobkerries were brought out and polished, and everything was made ready for the battle. Dombala donned his war garb and before nightfall the warriors had already started their war-dance. On through the dark hours they leapt and stamped, while the women and piccanins clapped their hands to keep in time with the ever-rising chanting.

But as the sun rose beyond the hills, the attackers could be seen creeping over the koppies towards the kraal. With a mighty shout the warriors of Dombala charged out, yelling their fierce war cry. The battle was on!

All morning it raged. Although the enemy numbered many more than the small tribe, the invaders were getting steadily beaten. The hearts of Dombala and the fine little impi filled with joy as they saw themselves becoming the victors.

But they did not feel happy for long. For, seeing his hordes were losing ground, the cruel chief sent at once for more warriors from his kraal.

"Alas!" cried Dombala, as he saw what was happening. "Now, my people, I think the end is near. For although you have fought bravely, when they and their helpers attack once again, I do not think we can hold out any longer."

And in the distance could be seen arriving hundreds upon hundreds of fresh warriors of the enemy, brandishing their assegais and shields in the air. On and on they came, only stopping to discuss plans with the remainder of the first attackers that had retreated.

The brave little tribe that had fought so well, with such splendid spirit, took up the best positions possible. Each man was determined to fight until he dropped, but their hearts were heavy when they thought of their wives and their piccanins.

But what was that?

Between the advancing enemy and Dombala's men, right round the huts, big plants had appeared out of the ground. Up they sprang, side by side, their large spiked leaves growing closely together, making an impassable wall.

The invaders came on, laughing scornfully when they saw the barrier forming. But more wonderful still, as they reached the green-spiked wall, tongues of fire darted out from the middle of the plants. One after another they threw out their curls of flame, filling the hearts of the boastful invaders with terror. A few more strides they advanced, but the fire scorched their black skins. They halted, blank amazement on their faces. Then, with a terrific yell of fear, they dropped their assegais and, turning tail, fled for their lives.

"Call the other small tribes, call the other small tribes!" shouted Dombala to his people, who were overjoyed at their deliverance by the good spirits in their hour of danger.

So, through the green wall that opened to let them out, the brave little tribe ran, gathering strength and numbers from friendly neighbours. So powerful did they grow, that by the time they came upon the enemy, they overpowered them completely. Then came the victorious return to the kraal, where they were troubled no more by enemy tribes.

And now, when you see the aloes growing up straight and proud on the koppies, remember how they first came – by the magic of the black gods who always protect their good people.

DID YOU KNOW?

The *aloe* is actually part of the lily family. There are more than 140 varieties of aloe in South Africa. They are succulents – all have fleshy leaves and can hold moisture for the plant to live on even during long spells of dry weather. Many of them have red flowers, and the "red-hot poker" is a common sight by South African roads. The different types range from the kokerboom (or quiver tree) in dry Namaqualand to the 15-metre tree *Aloe bainesii*, which grows in the forests north of East London. Some dried aloe leaves are used to make snuff, others can be eaten as a vegetable. Aloe leaves are also used to lessen the sting of the "blue-bottle" jelly-fish that floats ashore on our western beaches.

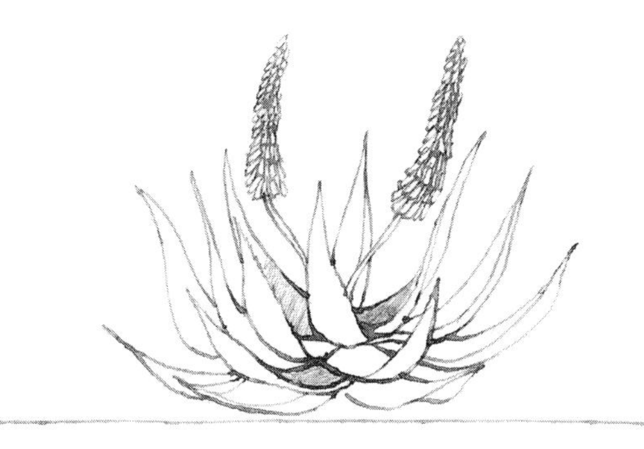

Klaus Kühne

Crocodile shoes

One wet, windy day as Mr Jelly was hurrying home from the Company's Gardens in Cape Town, he found he had a hole in his shoe that let the water in.

"What a nuisance," he muttered to himself, "I shall have to buy a new pair. But they will never be as comfortable as my old pair."

After breakfast the next morning, Mr Jelly fed the parrot and washed the dishes, and because it was a lovely sunny day he decided to walk into town. Bored with the shops in Adderley Street, he soon found himself in a narrow cobbled lane near the Castle.

"I don't remember walking down this lane

before," he thought. There were lots of quaint little shops on either side and Mr Jelly began looking out for one that sold shoes.

He passed a laundry, a bakery, a second-hand book shop and on the corner he saw a large, flat metal shoe swinging from a rusty bracket on the wall.

"Ah, a shoe shop," Mr Jelly said, pushing open the door.

A little bell tinkled as he stepped inside. Behind the counter stood the owner. Mr Jelly noticed that he had a pair of merry brown eyes and a big ginger moustache like a hairy caterpillar on his upper lip.

"Good morning to you, sir," said the man with a polite bow.

"Good morning," replied Mr Jelly. "I need a sturdy pair of brown shoes, size eight and a half."

The man snapped his fingers and immediately began rummaging among the shoe boxes on the shelves. Most of the boxes appeared to be empty and Mr Jelly wondered if there were any shoes in the shop at all.

Finally the man stood a rickety ladder against the wall and began searching among the dusty boxes on the very top shelf. At last he shook his head sadly.

"I don't seem to have any brown shoes in your size, sir."

Mr Jelly was about to say he'd go somewhere else for his shoes when the man continued, "I do, however, have a very smart pair of crocodile shoes in the store room that may fit you. I made them myself."

Mr Jelly sighed and glanced at his watch. It was taking a very long time to buy one pair of shoes. But then a pair of crocodile shoes sounded very smart indeed.

The man clambered down the ladder and disappeared behind a dusty green curtain at the back of the shop. Moments later he emerged with a large cardboard box in his hands.

Mr Jelly sat down and took off his shoes. The man with the ginger moustache slipped the new pair onto his feet and tied the laces firmly. They were the most comfortable shoes in the world. Even more comfortable than his old pair.

"Walk across the room and tell me how they feel," said the man with a grin.

Mr Jelly felt as if there were new life in his feet. It was almost as if the shoes were walking by themselves.

"I'll take them!" he said promptly.

The man with the ginger moustache wrapped the old pair up in brown paper and after paying for the crocodile shoes, Mr Jelly stepped jauntily into the street once more.

"I think I'll buy some lamb chops for lunch," Mr Jelly remarked as he heard the boom of the noonday gun from Signal Hill. It was only a short walk to the nearest butchery.

No sooner had he stepped into the butcher's shop, however, than his left foot suddenly shot out from underneath him and he found himself staggering helplessly towards the meat counter on one leg!

Then it was the turn of his right foot. It looked as if Mr Jelly was doing a strange sort of dance in the middle of the floor.

Mr Jelly was utterly amazed at his strange behaviour. He stared at his feet and gasped with surprise – his brand new shoes had turned into a pair of hungry crocodiles!

Now they were trying to reach a tasty leg of mutton that lay on top of the meat counter. The two crocodile shoes eagerly thrashed their scaly tails as they took turns in snapping hungrily at the mutton with their sharp, white teeth.

The butcher saw them and angrily flicked his apron at their snouts.

"Hey!" he shouted. "Get away from the meat, you two overgrown lizards."

Poor Mr Jelly felt very embarrassed and confused. On top of it all, he was getting terribly tired of hopping from one foot to the other.

"Quickly!" he gasped, handing the butcher some money. "Feed my shoes!"

The butcher cut two long strips of tripe and carefully fed them to the two hungry crocodile shoes.

They were not at all pleased at being offered tripe when they had set their hearts on mutton, but they quickly gobbled it all up.

When they had finished eating, Mr Jelly was able to sit down and catch his breath. But he didn't dare sit down for too long, in case his shoes should feel hungry again.

After a few minutes he rushed outside and clambered aboard a passing bus.

The ride back to his flat in Oranjezicht was a nightmare. The other passengers kept staring at his feet and pointing and giggling and nudging each other. Mr Jelly pretended not to notice.

He was very glad to get home. The more so because the two crocodile shoes started fighting each other, nearly tripping him up.

"These shoes will have to go back," he vowed as he sat down on his bed and started untying the laces. The shoes did not like this and snapped at his fingers.

There was nothing he could do but sleep with them on. Mr Jelly spent a very uncomfortable night while the shoes wriggled and squirmed and scratched without a break.

The next morning he rose early to return the troublesome shoes. He left in such a hurry that he forgot to feed the parrot or make himself breakfast. Mr Jelly wandered up and down the streets searching for the mysterious shoe shop. He peered in all the windows and asked directions, but nobody had heard of the shop. It had completely disappeared.

At midday, Mr Jelly was exhausted. He limped to the Gardens and sat down wearily on his favourite bench under a tall paperwood tree. How on earth was he to get rid of the troublesome crocodile shoes?

Then he had a bright idea. He rolled up his trouser legs above the knee and scrambled over the railings surrounding the lily pond. Then he slowly lowered his feet into the water. Very carefully he bent forward and untied the laces.

With a splish and a splosh and a flick of their tails the two crocodile shoes swam away and vanished among the floating water lilies.

Mr Jelly heaved a sigh of relief. At last he was rid of the crocodile shoes!

"I'll have my old pair resoled," he said, wiping his forehead with relief. "It's much safer!"

Dianne Stewart

Thekwane and Frog

One November morning, when all was quiet at the dam except for the gentle rustle of reeds and grasses, Frog emerged from his hiding-place in the mud.

Suddenly, the silence was disturbed by a "wek . . . wek . . . wek . . ." sound and Frog slid back into the warm mud. It was the voice of Thekwane, the big brown hamerkop bird, who flew down from the willow tree that stood with its branches resting gently in the dam. He by-passed the bulrushes with their brown candle flowers and landed at the water's edge.

Closing his large wings, he began slosh-sloshing in the mud with his feet. The air became alive with the sound and vibration of the little insects that live close to any dam. He stood on one foot and scratched in the mud with the other, uncovering the worms, crabs, insects and frogs that were his food.

When they heard him, all the little dam-dwellers remained very still or moved away to escape him.

"Run!" said the land crabs to each other as they heard his cry. With their eyes on stalks, they scuttled quickly away.

"We are not afraid," said the mosquitoes, as they buzzed through the air looking for warm-blooded creatures.

The worms remained silent and still in their muddy holes at the dam edge.

Frog, too, did not move as Thekwane waded in the shallow water among the reeds.

Suddenly he heard a strange, shuffling sound coming from the reeds. He surfaced from the mud to see Thekwane struggling frantically to free his foot from a tangle of reeds and grasses. After a few minutes Thekwane had freed himself, but was hopping along the water's edge in a great deal of pain.

Frog noticed that Thekwane was unable to stand on his right leg. He hopped closer to the large bird and said, "Please, Thekwane, don't eat me. If we are friends, then I can find food for you."

The hamerkop bird hesitated for a moment, then replied, "Thank you, kind Frog. Please be quick. I am hungry."

The sun peered through a gap in the clouds and warmed the muddy shallows where Thekwane stood watching as the little brown frog tried to find food for him. Just ahead of him, a dragon-fly's transparent wings glistened in the sunlight. Frog flicked out his long tongue and curled it around the dragon-fly's body. It clung fast to his tongue until it was passed on to the hungry Thekwane.

"Here, Thekwane," said Frog, eager to please. "You may feast on this dragon-fly."

Thekwane gobbled it greedily.

"Find me some more food," he said. "I am still hungry."

Frog set off and was quite a distance away when Thekwane heard a rustling sound in the long grass behind him. He caught sight of the slimy green snake called Saba, and with the aid of his strong left leg, he took to the air with a squeaky cry. He flap-flapped

his large brown wings and allowed the air currents to carry him towards his nest in the willow tree.

Frog had seen him take to the air and watched with envy from the ground. He suddenly realized that he was earth-bound and he longed to be a creature of the air.

"I wish I could fly," said Frog, sadly.

Thekwane came to rest on a branch at the top of the willow tree and shook his body dry. Frog slid back into the mud and disappeared from sight. His skin was the same colour as the mud, and he could not easily be seen.

Warm November days came and went. The dragon-flies continued patrolling the edge of the dam, marking out their territory. The mosquitoes buzzed, and the swallows were frequent visitors, quenching their thirst with the sweet waters of the dam.

Frog went on wishing to fly until one morning he heard the sound of "wek . . . wek . . . wek" coming closer and closer and Thekwane landed among the reeds in search of a crab. His injured leg had healed and once again he began slosh-sloshing in the mud. He found a juicy crab, ate it, and stood in the murky water, dipping his long black bill to drink. He then spread his broad brown wings and preened himself.

Hidden in the mud at the edge of the reeds was Frog. He surfaced with a "glug, glug" sound and took an enormous leap towards Thekwane. This movement attracted the bird's attention, and he looked forward to renewing his friendship with the frog.

Alas! It had also caught the eye of the long green snake, Saba. He had been watching Frog from the tall green grass next to the reeds. Quietly, without taking his eyes off him, the snake slithered between the blades of green grass and headed towards the reeds. He had slept all through the winter, curled up in a hole. Now that it was summer and the weather was warmer, he had awoken from his long sleep and was hungry. He was very hungry.

Thekwane watched as the snake moved towards the frog. Snakes can slither faster than frogs can hop. Saba was about to strike when Thekwane leaned forward and grabbed Frog in his long black beak.

With his long legs, Thekwane took to the air with Frog safely in his beak. Frog was

dazed, but Thekwane calmed him. "Do not be afraid. You are safe now."

They flew across the dam and landed. How different the view was from the other side of the dam.

"Stay in the mud and keep away from the reeds and long grass," Thekwane advised.

Frog was greatly relieved to be out of the way of the snake. "You have saved my life," he croaked. "I am so grateful to you."

"You were kind enough to find food for me when I had hurt my leg," said Thekwane.

It was midday and the sun shone brightly. The dam waters glistened. Wind rustled through the reeds and the willow trees swayed gently.

"I can see now, that I am happier on the ground," said Frog. "Like the swallows, you are able to swoop down, have a drink of water, then fly high again into the air. I can satisfy my thirst by just soaking in water. Away from water I would shrivel and die."

"Living in water wouldn't suit me," said Thekwane. "I hate to get my feathers wet, and that is why I wade in shallow water and have such long, long legs."

After a while, Thekwane flew back across the dam to his nest in the willow tree. Frog hopped happily to the water's edge and disappeared under the warm brown mud. He felt safe now. He felt proud to be a frog.

DID YOU KNOW?

The *hamerkop* (or hammer-head bird) gets its name from the crest of feathers which makes its head look like a hammer. Its Zulu name, used in this story, is iThekwane. The hamerkop lives mostly on small water creatures. Like the magpie, it loves picking up shiny objects and anything with bright colours, which it builds into its untidy nest. It might even fly off with a piece of your clothing – so watch out!

Juliet Marais Louw

Holiday for Mother

"I can't go on holiday,"
said Mrs le Roux.
"None of the family
would know what to do.
Dad would have no breakfast,
Bill would miss the bus
(he never does his homework
unless I make a fuss);
Nellie'd leave her sandwiches,
Sally wouldn't eat;
she'd drop her history notebook
at the corner of the street.
And when the fridge is empty,
who would order meat?
Everybody, everything
stops without a mother –
how can I go anywhere
to visit my brother?

I can't go on holiday,
who would feed the cat?
Who'd pay the light bill
and things like that?
I can't go on holiday –
there's another reason:
I couldn't leave the family
in the rugby season.
Who'd apply a plaster
when Frikkie has a blister?
How can I go anywhere
to visit my sister?

I couldn't go to Bloemfontein
and leave them all alone,
nor yet to Port Elizabeth
to stay with Cousin Joan;
I wouldn't even spend a week
with Ouma on the farm –
I'd never go on holiday
and let them come to harm."

Jay Heale

The little hare

The drinking pool of the animals had plenty of water, but it was cloudy and muddy. So Big Lion, as king of the beasts, ordered that no one should drink there until the water had settled and was clear.

All the animals sighed and obeyed. All, that is, except Hare, who liked to have his own way. Besides, he was thirsty. So that night, when the other animals were asleep, he crept down to the edge of the pool and drank all he wanted. This stirred up the cloudy mud in the water. Hare looked around and he saw Dassie sleeping near, so he smeared mud all over Dassie's face and paws, to make it look as if he had disobeyed Big Lion's orders.

The next morning, in the grey light before the sun came, Big Lion marched straight for the pool and all the other animals marched with him. They stopped – Crrah! – at the edge. Once again the water was cloudy and muddy.

Big Lion was angry. "Who has been drinking our water?" he growled.

Hare gave a lickety-hoppity-jump and pointed to Dassie. "Father Lion – look, look!" he said. "There is the one who drank your water! There is the one who muddied the pool. See the mud on his face and paws."

"No!" said Dassie, quivering and shivering. "It wasn't me. I never did it."

But Big Lion would not listen. "Beat him on the back with a bamboo cane!" he ordered. And they did. Bam – Boo – Bam – Boo! Dassie shrieked and squeaked.

All this while Hare was hugging himself with glee at his cleverness. Dassie had been beaten instead of him! He was so full of himself that he couldn't keep his mouth shut. A quick look around. Nobody near. He lay on his back and laughed and laughed. "I drank the water, but Dassie took the blame! Dassie got the beating and I got the fame!"

But flying overhead was Grey Lourie, the Go-Away bird, whose sharp hearing caught what Hare was boasting. Lourie flew to Big Lion. "Kweh, kwaay!" said Lourie. "You must hear what Hare is boasting." So Big Lion sent for Hare and asked him what he had been boasting about.

Hare saw no point in trying to hide what he had done, so he sang once again, "I drank the water, but Dassie took the blame! Dassie got the beating and I got the fame!" Then he jumped up and ran away as fast as he could – scurry hurry – with all the other animals after him.

They had almost caught him when he dashed into a narrow crack in a rock far too small for them to follow. But in his hurry he had left one of his long ears sticking out, which Jackal managed to grab. Though Jackal pulled as hard as he could, and all the other animals pulled Jackal, they could not drag Hare out of the crack in the rock. At last they gave up and left him there, with his ear painfully scratched and torn.

When the last tail was out of sight, the little hare crept cautiously out, and who should he see but the dassie. Boldly he went up to him, lickety-hoppity-jump, and said, "Well, my good Dassie, you can see that I have had a beating as well as you."

But Dassie was still sore and sulky, and did not want to chat. He said coldly, "It isn't fair. You muddied the water and you made it look as if I did. I shall call the other animals so they can catch you."

"My good Dassie," said the Hare, chuckling to himself, "forget about all that. I have such an exciting secret to tell you. Do you know what to do to escape being burnt to death?"

"No, I don't," said Dassie, who was just as inquisitive as all animals.

"We begin by digging a hole. Come and help me."

So the stupid dassie and the crafty little hare dug and dug in the hard dry ground till their paws were sore. Then Hare said, "Next we must make a fire in the hole." So they both collected dry thorns and dead branches and lit quite a large fire.

When it was burning brightly, Hare said to Dassie, "Dassie, my friend, throw me into the fire, and when you hear my fur crackling and I call 'Itchi, Itchi!', then quickly pull me out."

So Dassie threw Hare into the fire – Waeooh! No sooner did Hare begin to feel the heat of the flames than he took some green gonna leaves he had picked beforehand and pushed them in the centre of the fire where they crackled loudly – Scrick-Scrack! Then he called, "Itchi, Itchi! Dassie, be quick. Can't you hear my skin crackling?"

Dassie pulled him out of the fire as fast as he could. "Now it's your turn," said Hare, and he threw Dassie into the fire – Waeooh! And when Dassie felt the heat of the flames, he too cried out, "Itchi, Itchi! I am burning. Pull me out quick!"

Hare decided that the fire still wasn't quite hot enough for the plan he had in mind, so he pulled Dassie out. Giggling and chuckling, Hare said, "Now let's try it again. You throw me in the fire." So Dassie threw him in – Waeooh! Almost straight away Hare started to cry, "Listen to my skin crackling!" and the gonna leaves once again went Scrick-Scrack! "Itchi, Itchi! Pull me out!" shouted Hare, and Dassie did so. "See?" he said. "You could hear my skin crackling, but I'm not burnt at all. Now it's your turn again." And with a shout of laughter at Dassie's bewilderment, he threw Dassie into the fire, which was now blazing white-hot.

Immediately Dassie cried, "Itchi, Itchi! I am burning. Pull me out!"

But Hare only laughed even more and said, "No, no – you stay where you are. It's your fault anyway. Why did you let me throw you in? Didn't you know that fire burns?" And within a few minutes there was nothing left of the dassie but a few bones.

When the fire was out and the ashes cold, Hare picked up one of the bones, carved it into a flute, and piped this song,

"Pi-i-pi-i – My pipe is done –
Dassie was a silly one!
Pi-i-pi-i – The fire was hot –
I burnt him up and that's his lot!"

Hare sang this everywhere he went. But even he became tired of his own boasting, so he went back to Big Lion and promised to behave and to make himself useful. But he hadn't forgotten his old tricks.

One day Hare said, "Oh, Father Lion, chasing after animals to catch them must be a terribly tiring way of getting your food. Shall I show you a much easier way?"

"What is it?" asked Big Lion.

"You must dig a hole, and then you must lie in it and pretend to be dead."

So Big Lion dug with his front paws and scrabbled with his back paws in the hard dry earth, and when the hole was big enough he lay down in it. Hare jumped up

on a rock, lickety-hoppity-jump, blew a merry tune on his flute, and shouted,

"Pi-i-pi-i – All come and see –
Lion is dead, so peace will be."

As soon as they heard his song, all the animals came running, for many of them had been too frightened ever to take a close look at Big Lion when he was alive. Hare welcomed them all and sang,

"Pi-i-pi-i – Come this way, please.
Lion is dead – feel quite at ease!"

And he guided them all inside the great enclosure of tightly packed thorn bushes where Big Lion had his lair.

Last of all the animals came Monkey with her baby clinging to her back. She followed them to the hole where Big Lion was lying. As no one seemed to be looking, she plucked a piece of grass and tickled Big Lion's bottom with it. It *did* tickle, and Big Lion couldn't help twitching. Itch-twitch!

Monkey cried out, "Hold on tight, my

baby! We're going. What sort of dead body twitches when it's tickled?" And she dashed off in a fright with her baby.

Hare pulled spiky thorn bushes into the entrance, to shut Big Lion's lair completely. When the thorns were tight-packed, with heavy stones against them to prevent them being moved, Hare shouted out, "Now!" And Big Lion bounded out of the hole and tore the other animals into tiny little bite-sized pieces.

But Big Lion kept all the best bits for himself, and only gave Hare the gristly bits he didn't like. So Hare was annoyed and decided to get his own back. He knew by now how easy it was to fool Big Lion, so he planned to do it again.

"What an idea!" he cried, hitting his head with a paw – Fding! – as if the idea had flown out of the blue sky. "Father Lion, let us build a hut."

To Big Lion it seemed a sensible plan. So Big Lion planted the stakes in the ground and tied them together with wild vines to make the rounded roof. Then Big Lion wove the wattles in and out to make the walls. And when they were ready to start on the roof, Hare told Big Lion, "You climb up on top, while I go inside. We'll weave the roof together." So Big Lion climbed on the criss-cross branches which made the roof, and Hare scurried into the shady hut and called out, "Ready, Father Lion! You start."

Big Lion took a bendy wattle stick and pushed it through from the top. Hare took it and called out, "Stay there while I weave it through and pass it back." As he was speaking, he poked the stick up through the roof and jabbed Big Lion right in his tail.

"Grr-owf," yelped Big Lion. "What was that?"

"Oh, it's just a branch sticking out. Don't move. I'm just fixing it," said Hare, but of course he had done it on purpose as he wanted to fix Big Lion's tail so that he wouldn't be able to move. Carefully he wound the bendy stick round and round, and tied it tight with wild vine. Then he went outside and quietly began to eat Big Lion's dinner, while all Lion could do was watch and roar with rage. Growl! Howl!

When he had eaten all he could, Hare took out his bone flute and started to play and sing,

"Pi-i-pi-i – Come, stormy gale!
Fill the sky with rain and hail!"

Before long, the sky darkened, lightning flashed, thunder blundered, and huge hailstones beat upon the whole countryside and on that hut in particular. Hare hopped smartly inside the hut for safety and called out, "Father Lion, don't waste time. Come down and eat with me." But there was no answer, not even a growl or a whimper, for the hailstones had killed Big Lion dead.

DID YOU KNOW?

The clever hare in the story is a sort of relation of *Brer Rabbit*. In many African animal stories, the hare is the clever trickster. When Africans were taken over to America in the 18th century, many of them as slaves, they went on telling stories of this kind. But as hares weren't so common in the southern states, they made their hare a rabbit instead, and they called him Brer (or Brother) Rabbit.

Theodora Wynn

Chikalulu

Chikalulu was walking along the road near to the general store when his eye was caught by something very different in the window. In the centre of all the jumble of blankets, hats and paraffin stoves something glowed and sparkled and it looked like . . . well . . . it *was* an egg, but it was bright red and shone like the setting sun.

Chikalulu stared in astonishment. He had seen many kinds of eggs: those from the long-legged hens around his mother's hut, small ones in birds' nests in the trees, even a crocodile's eggs buried in the sand, but he had never seen a *red* egg.

He took another surprised look into the store window and then set off in a little hopping trot back to his home in the valley.

When he arrived, his mother was busy cooking the midday meal and shooing away the hens which were pecking around her feet.

"Why are you so late, my son?" she asked crossly. "Come at once, for your father is looking for you."

Chikalulu was much too excited to care about who was looking for him and burst out with the story of the wonderful egg. His mother listened with very little patience and when he had finished, she said, "Chikalulu, you would be far better off doing your school work or helping with the cows than running about making up bad lies to tell me."

Chikalulu's eyes opened wide and he felt sad. Although his mother had scolded him for many things in his eight years of life, never before had she accused him of lying.

"But, Mother, it is the truth," he said. "I really saw this egg in the store window. It is there for all to see. Will you not go and see it for yourself?"

"Am I to make a fool of myself for the sake of a lazy little boy who makes pictures in his head?" she asked, and Chikalulu ran off thinking she was probably angry because his big brother, who wanted to go to live in the big city, was causing her a lot of worry.

As Chikalulu kicked stones along the path with his stubby toes, he saw his father coming back from the fields. Rushing up to him he began to tell the story of the shining egg. His father did not slow down, so Chikalulu hopped along beside him speaking in a very breathless voice. Suddenly his father spoke and the way his voice sounded made Chikalulu feel quite afraid.

"What is this fable that you tell me?" he roared. "Do I have to be the father of a liar as well as a gadabout?" Chikalulu did not know what a gadabout was, but he felt his father must be speaking about his brother.

"Please, Father, it is true . . . come to see it," he begged, but his father paid no attention and went into the cooking hut demanding his food.

Later, when Chikalulu went down the path to drive the cows home for milking, he sang his usual little song, but today it was sad-sounding, and instead of hopping like a spring hare he walked slowly like the tortoise in his heavy shell. Tortoises lay eggs, too, thought Chikalulu and began to think about the egg again.

Soon he was driving the cows back to the place of milking and as he went he saw the umfundisi, the local teacher, arrive wearing his black coat and hat. He entered the cooking hut and Chikalulu knew that he had come to speak about the problem of his elder brother.

Chikalulu sat down outside the door of the hut. Soon his mother came out and told him it was time to eat and to be very respectful as the umfundisi was there. He sat quietly watching and listening as they ate, and when the umfundisi had finished his talk, Chikalulu began eagerly to tell him about the red egg. He could see that his father and mother were shocked with him for mentioning it, but he kept on with the story, hoping that he would be believed.

The umfundisi seemed a little absent-minded as he stopped and walked out of

the hut, and he patted Chikalulu's head as he said farewell to the parents.

As soon as he was out of sight, Chikalulu's father picked him up and spanked him. Chikalulu cried out, but his father said that he was being spanked for telling lies in front of the umfundisi.

The next day Chikalulu had almost given up thinking about the wonderful egg, when his mother called to tell him that she was going to fetch muti from the Oldest Aunt and that he was to come with her. Chikalulu liked to go to the home of the Oldest Aunt, for she had so many strange and sometimes smelly things hung outside her hut and left to dry in the sun. There were birds and lizards and even parts of a leopard hung there. The Oldest Aunt once said that the leopard muti would make him brave and strong, and Chikalulu wondered if she would allow him to have some now.

After his mother had bought some powdered roots, she put them into her apron pocket and turning to the aunt said, "My Old One, perhaps there is something that you could give a bad child who sees strange things in his mind?" She looked at Chikalulu, not *very* crossly, as she was always a little bit nicer to him after his father had scolded him, and drew him to her side.

"What is this thing that the child has seen?" asked the Oldest Aunt in a voice that sounded like the bell in the church up on the hill, a good sound but a little cracked.

"Please," he said, "it is a wonderful sight, an egg as big as my two hands and shining like the light on the back of the city bus."

"Hmm," crackled the Oldest Aunt, "and what sort of bird could have made this wondrous egg? A guinea-fowl or perhaps a magic eagle?"

Chikalulu hung his head and looked foolish. "I do not know, my aunt," he said.

"Then we must go to the store and see for ourselves," she replied.

"Would you encourage the child in his stories?" asked Chikalulu's mother in anger. "He has told this tale to his father and myself and even to the umfundisi, and there is enough trouble in our family without this child being listened to by the wisest woman in the district."

"Perhaps it is because of this wisdom that I shall pay heed to the words of a child," announced the Oldest Aunt. "Let us go."

Chikalulu's face shone like a lamp and he danced along next to his mother. They set off down the road at a slow pace, for the hair of the Oldest Aunt was white and her steps were very slow.

They had walked a very short distance when they met Chikalulu's father, who greeted them and said, "Where does this road take you, Old One?"

"We go to see the egg the child speaks of," she replied.

Chikalulu's father looked very angry, but he did not dare to argue with the wise old woman, so he joined the little party and they all went on together.

Soon they came to a tarred road where the cars and buses rushed by, and there, sitting at the bus stop, was the umfundisi.

"Where do you go – so many of you?" he asked, surprised to see the old woman so far from her hut, with the three others following her.

"We go to see the egg that the child speaks of," she repeated. The umfundisi looked puzzled.

"Do you not remember the story he told you in the cooking hut?" asked Chikalulu's mother.

The umfundisi smiled. "Of course, now I remember," he said, "but I gave it little heed as I thought it was the chatter of a young one. But now I, too, will come with you to the store to see."

Chikalulu was very excited at the idea of all the grown-ups going to the store with him.

But suddenly he thought how bad it would be if the storekeeper had sold the egg – it would seem that he had been making up the story after all. Then, surely, he would have the worst punishment of his life! His heart began to beat a bit faster and he looked forward anxiously to see if the glitter of red was still there among all the other goods in the store window.

But he could see nothing.

Nearer and nearer they came to the store and Chikalulu could wait no longer. He darted forward to peer past the crowd of people gossiping outside the store. Yes . . . the egg was still there! Chikalulu sighed with relief, and he turned to await the slow arrival of the Oldest Aunt and his family.

The people stood aside as the old woman moved towards the window and watched with respect and curiosity. She peered into the window and then cried, "There it is, just as the small one said," and turned to watch the faces of Chikalulu's parents and the umfundisi. To Chikalulu's surprise the umfundisi began to laugh.

"It is true," he chuckled. "We have all forgotten that it is the time of the year for the Easter egg. In our church we shall remember that Jesus died for us, and many Christian children eat chocolate eggs as a symbol of a new life and a new beginning. That egg, my friends, is made of sweet stuff. It came from no bird and is wrapped in a wonderful shining paper."

Chikalulu had learnt about Jesus in church, so he crouched down by the window to gaze at the egg.

Suddenly he turned and saw that all his people were standing in a huddle, and then the umfundisi walked forward and gave Chikalulu a handful of coins. "Here, my son," he said. "Take this money and go to the storekeeper and ask for the egg. Your father and mother, the Oldest Aunt and I have each given a little that you may buy the egg as a reward for telling the truth without fear."

Chikalulu took the money and ran into the store. The storekeeper took the egg from the window and gave it to him.

Chikalulu carried the egg home with great care and it was many days before he could start to eat it, and even now he has the lovely piece of shining red paper hung on the wall of the hut where he sleeps. He calls it the skin of the Red Egg.

DID YOU KNOW?

The *egg* has been an important sign of new life for thousands of years. It was probably brought into the celebrations for Easter to remind people that Jesus broke out of the tomb in the same way that a chick breaks out of the egg.

The name "Easter" comes from Eostre, the goddess of spring, worshipped by the Vikings in northern Europe. The return of spring and the re-birth of the plants was celebrated by giving specially coloured eggs as presents. In some countries they were hard-boiled, and even rolled down the hillsides with children chasing after!

Hélaine Gollom

A first-class fish called Clifton

A small boat drifted across the water of False Bay. Kosie, one of the fishermen at Kalk Bay harbour, was going out for his daily haul. This day seemed no different from any other because, after all, he had been doing this for twenty years.

The fish were few and life was tough for a fisherman like Kosie. What was happening beneath the waves not even he could tell. Kosie narrowed his eyes, smiled a sunburnt smile and pulled his line once again through the water. All alone, far out to sea, with many hungry mouths to feed back home, he waited, wondering what the catch would be like that day.

At that moment something hit the boat. Kosie staggered and fell, but hung onto his fishing line. A giant fish burst into mid-air. Only then did Kosie realise he was about to make the biggest catch of his life.

He sang for joy as he hauled the huge fish on board, admiring its gleaming silver-green scales and strong fins. Into his biggest bucket it went, so he could take it home alive.

All the peace and stillness of the ocean vanished as he headed towards the harbour. On the quay, noisy crowds of Cape fishermen, families, children and numerous onlookers gathered around, pushing and shoving, trying to catch sight of the boat. Excitement filled the air.

"Get back, get back!" shouted Kosie, and everyone stepped back on to each other's toes. With the help of the other fishermen, he hauled out the fish on to the quay. Scales and salt water splashed everywhere.

Kosie's great moment had arrived. Beaming proudly and delightedly he lifted the giant fish out of the boat. He held the fish high for everyone to see, and waited for someone to buy it.

Now, Mr Campbell, a photographer from California, and his wife were having a lovely holiday in South Africa. They had been the first to spot Kosie and his boat coming into the harbour. Mr Campbell was most excited about the boats and the fish. Mrs Campbell could not understand her husband's love of the sea, and she found fish slimy and disagreeable. Mr Campbell was boisterous and friendly. He never stopped taking pictures with his new camera. Boats and fishermen made good pictures.

Then he saw the fine fish that Kosie had caught, and he decided to buy it. Prices meant nothing to him, as he had never bought a fish before in his life. So he offered a very large sum of money, and Mrs Campbell groaned.

Kosie knew he must sell the fish, and he was most happy at the price he had been paid. But still he was filled with sorrow. He realised the beauty and majesty of the creature he had just sold. All his pride lay in the fish which to him was like a prize for all his hard years of fishing. He wanted to have the satisfaction of putting the fish back in the sea to complete his happiness.

So his knees went weak as he handed the fish over to Mr Campbell and took the money. These Americans would not understand his affection and admiration for this

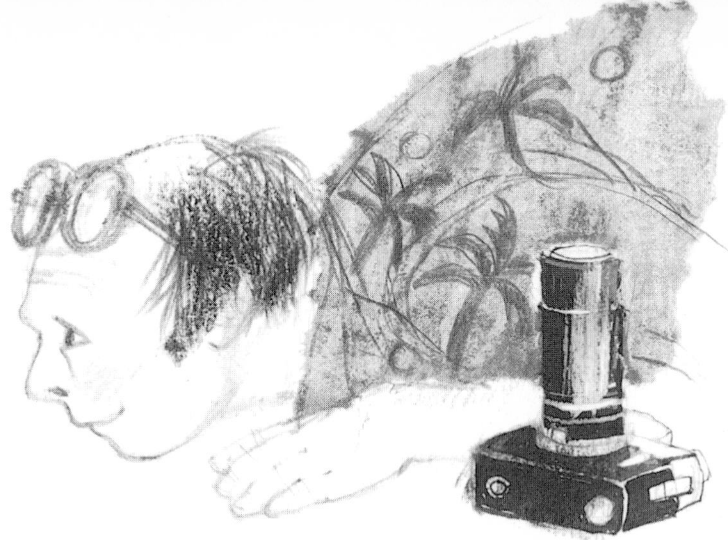

fish. First they would eat one side, and then the other. He felt ashamed.

"My goodness!" protested Mrs Campbell. "What *are* we going to do with that fish?"

"You will see," said Mr Campbell, much to his wife's dismay. She was secretly afraid of the large creature.

"We can't possibly take it back to the hotel. What will everybody say if they see us with this slimy creature?"

Mr Campbell ignored his wife's protests and took a closer look at the fish. "Why!" he exclaimed. "It's still alive!" A broad smile lit up his red face. "It would be a shame if it died. It looks so gentle and friendly." Already Mr Campbell began to look sad.

He fetched a bucket and gave it to a fisherman, who filled it with water and put the fish in it. "I shall name it Clifton," Mr Campbell decided, "after that pretty bay we visited yesterday. Clifton the Fish – that sounds good." He beamed with pride.

Mr Campbell started taking photographs.

Click! Click!

"Stop that at once! Look at all the film you are wasting," protested Mrs Campbell.

Without a word, Mr Campbell carried on taking pictures, pretending he hadn't heard. Then, to his amazement, the fish rolled out of the bucket right at Mr Campbell's feet, leant back against a stone and appeared to smile. What a picture! Mr Campbell remained speechless. Never had he found such a helpful model. "How beautiful!" he said, enthusiastically. "And how unusual!"

Clifton the fish was really doing his best. His extra size had given him extra brains too. He tried to lift his body higher, but there is a limit to what a fish can do out of water. He slipped and fell to the ground, panting.

Click!

With genuine concern, Mr Campbell dropped his camera. He bent down and tried to pick up the fish. The scales, smooth and perfect, glittered in the sunlight. Alas, it slipped out of his hands and fell back to the ground.

He looked around for someone to help, but the crowd had moved away to the other end of the harbour, where another boat had come in. There were only Mr Campbell and his wife. And there was poor Clifton, fainting from lack of water. The film unit back in Hollywood would pay him enough money to find many more fishes, but none would be like Clifton. He was truly magnificent. There was only one way to save him.

"Come on, my dear," said Mr Campbell to his wife. "You must help me carry Clifton back to our hotel."

She complained every bit of the way, but she did help. That was how Clifton ended up in the hotel bath, swimming in buckets of sea water. Another fine picture.

Click! Click! Click!

Mr Campbell looked at Clifton gratefully. "I believe that tomorrow I shall put you back into the sea," he said, smiling at the fish.

The next morning, Kosie returned to the harbour. He was feeling very sad until he saw Mr Campbell, who was still busy taking photographs of Clifton. Kosie gaped in surprise. "Why – the great fish is still alive!" he cried, and rushed down to where Mr Campbell stood.

Kosie was even more surprised when Mr Campbell said, "Ah! I have been waiting for you. Please will you put this wonderful fish in your boat, take him out, and put him back in the sea?"

Overjoyed, Kosie stammered, "I will indeed be happy to do this. I was so proud of this fish. He was the biggest catch of my life, and I have grown to like him. Thank you for giving me the chance to do this. It is a perfect idea. You will be my friend forever."

Mrs Campbell was most relieved to see Kosie get into his boat with Clifton the fish and get ready to go out to sea. She had had enough of the whole affair. But Mr Campbell was very sad.

"Why is it," he said, puzzled, "that the hardest thing in the world is to say goodbye? If I kept Clifton, he would surely die. He needs to be with his own kind."

Click!

Clifton's body shimmered in the bucket as he gazed affectionately at Mr Campbell. He looked as if he knew he was soon to be free.

"What an extraordinary fish," muttered Mr Campbell. "Extraordinary. Goodbye, Clifton!"

Kosie sailed swiftly out of the harbour, while Mr Campbell watched mournfully from the quay, sniffing a little. "I am glad that Clifton is free, but I do miss him so," he thought.

When Kosie returned to Kalk Bay harbour, he felt so sorry for Mr Campbell that he decided to give him a present. "Look what I have just caught!" he shouted, happily. And he hauled out a large, waving crayfish, its black pincers snapping dangerously.

Mrs Campbell took one look and fainted in a heap on the quay.

"No offence, madam," cried Kosie, pouring a bucket of sea water on her head to revive her.

"Please," she wept, shivering in a pool of water, "no more fish!"

"Never refuse a gift, my dear," said Mr Campbell, taking out his camera and eyeing the crayfish with interest. "Never refuse a gift."

And far out at sea, Clifton wagged his tail in agreement. He had received the greatest gift of all – his life and his freedom.

DID YOU KNOW?

Fishes breathe oxygen just as we do, but they have a special system. That curving flap at the side of a fish's head contains the gills. There are four gills, and they look red because of the blood flowing inside them. The fish takes in water through its mouth and pumps it out over the gills, which take the oxygen out of the water and into the fish's blood-stream. If you see a fish gasping in your home aquarium, it will be because the tank is too crowded and there isn't enough oxygen in the water. The air that you and I breathe contains thirty times as much oxygen as there is in water. So fish have to work hard to pump water through their gills. A tiny minnow, even when resting, pumps its gills about 150 times each minute. When we are resting, we breathe only twelve times a minute.

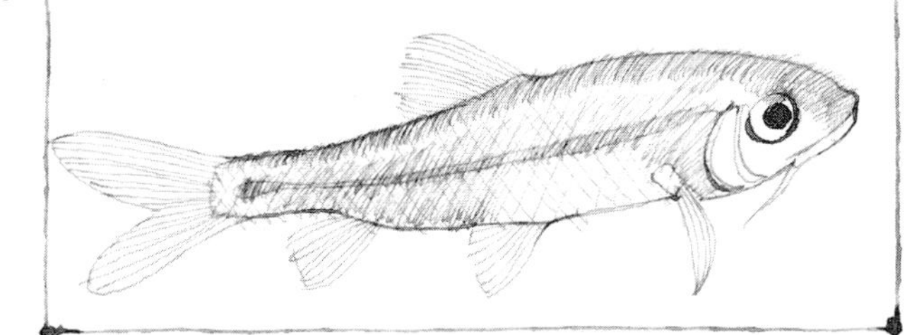

Philip de Vos

Poems

DODO

Way down in Mauritius
the dodo was delicious.
And that is why I think
that bird is now extink.

LADYBIRD

Pretty,
pretty
ladybird
with your spots
and polka dots –
rest a while
on my lapel,
and my day
will turn out well.

TWO PORCUPINES

Two porcupines
are worse than one;
meeting them
is not much fun.
Heed my words:
Beware, beware!
Two are such
a prickly pair!

THE HUNGRY HIPPO

Sixty-seven beetles
sitting on a spot . . .
A hungry hippo came along
and gobbled up the lot.

A LITTLE FISH TALE

I read somewhere that fishes cry
every time their kinsfolk die.
What is sea, and what is ocean?
Little drops of fish emotion.

GRANNY

Granny won't wear curlers,
Granny won't wear frocks,
Granny's fond of frothy beer
and whisky on the rocks.
Granny's never sad nor glum,
Granny's mad for bubblegum.
Here comes Granny chew chew chew –
hop skip jump at ninety-two!

Klaus Kühne

Wallet the pelican

Wallet the pelican lived with his family on the shore of a small lake near Swakopmund, on the dry desert coast of Namibia. Every day they went fishing. Grandfather Pelican flew in front and Wallet flew at the very back because he was the youngest.

Wallet muttered to himself as he flew:

"Silly old sea,
stupid old dunes,
boring old lake."

He was tired of being the youngest pelican. He was tired of flying behind everyone else.

One night Wallet decided to fly away by himself. "I'll find another lake, far away. A much nicer lake. And I'll build my own nest and catch fish when I feel like it, and I won't fly behind anyone else ever again."

Early the next morning, Wallet left the colony and flew south. He soon found a fine thermal wind current and soared high into the sky. Below he could see the vast, hot Namib desert and the cold, blue sea.

A short while later, he spotted a lake fringed with thick green reeds. He slowly spiralled down for a closer look. It was a perfect new home. There were lots of other birds nesting there, but no pelicans.

"Time for my breakfast," thought Wallet as he swooped in low over the water. His keen eyes spotted a small shoal of fish near the edge of the lake. He splashed down into the water and briskly paddled towards the fish. They were so bewildered that it took no time at all for him to scoop them up in his pouch.

Wallet found a shady spot and ate them all up. When he had finished, he plodded around the shoreline admiring the pattern his large, webbed feet made in the wet sand. It was more fun than wading around with the rest of the family and having to share his catch.

A few nights later, Wallet heard a strange rumbling sound. He slowly opened one eye and peered in the direction of the noise. It was too dark to see anything and the rumbling sound soon stopped. Wallet went back to sleep again.

It was only when he was fishing, later the next day, that Wallet discovered what the rumbling sound had brought. Spreading over the surface of the lake was a shimmering rainbow. It was oil and it came from a large pile of rubbish that had been dumped into the lake. Some dead fish, their white bellies glistening in the sun, floated on top of the water.

Dented tins, old motor car tyres, a rusty refrigerator and plastic bags full of evil-smelling rotting food had been dumped on the shore, where they crushed the reeds and spilled into the lake.

Angry, frightened birds were fluttering about where their nests had been broken and torn down.

A foul smell hung in the air.

Wallet stuck his beak into the water. It tasted horrible! He was surprised that the liquid which made such a beautiful pattern on the water should taste so bad.

As the days went by, Wallet noticed there

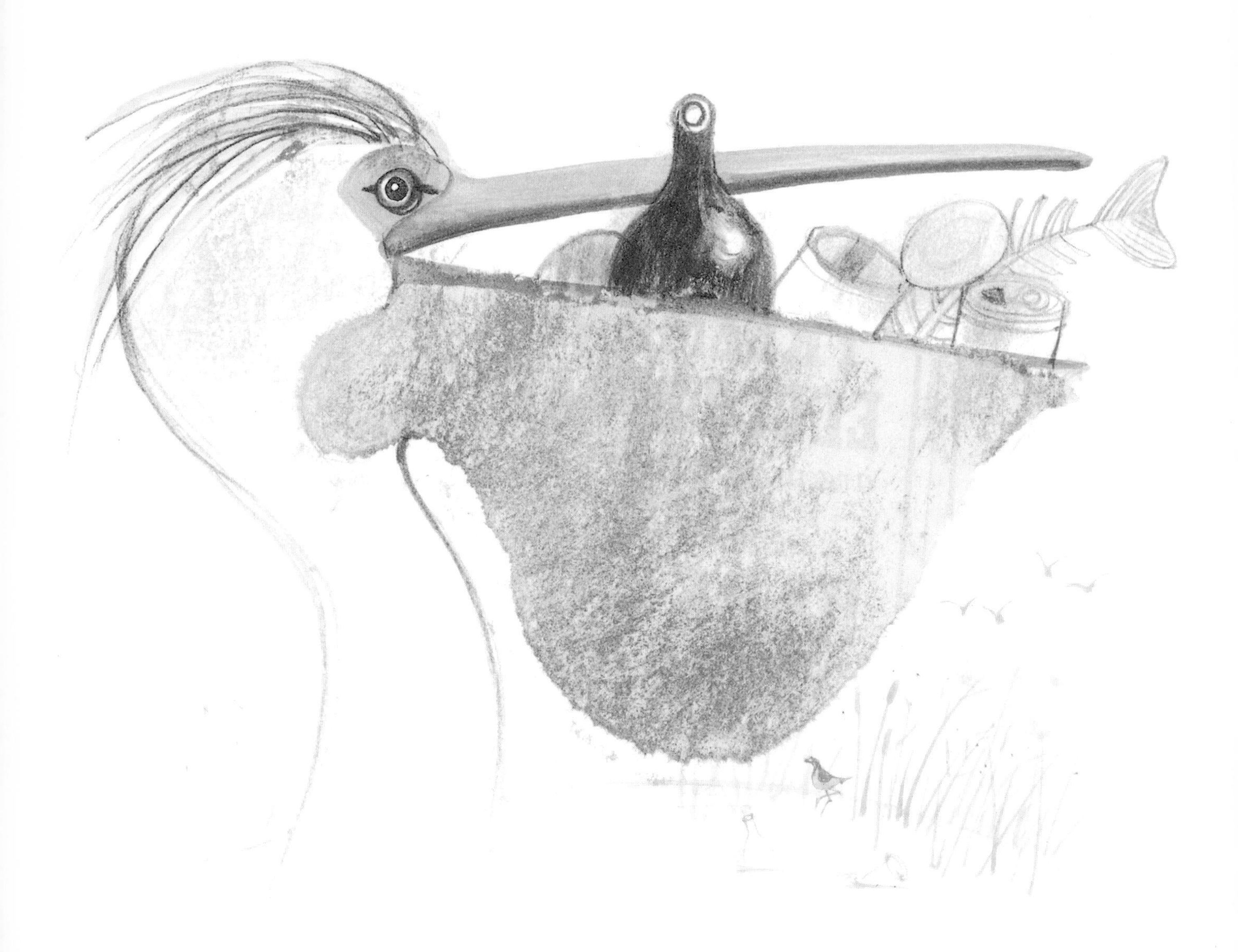

were more dead fish, and soon the whole of the lake which had been so attractive was covered with oil and floating rubbish.

He looked at his spoilt lake. "Perhaps I can get rid of this rubbish," he said to himself. But none of the other birds could help him. So he decided he would have to do it himself.

Wallet started picking up the rubbish. He filled the pouch under his beak with old tins and flew into the desert, where he dropped his load behind a high red sand dune. It was very hard work, and harder as he became more tired.

After three days of flying load after load of rubbish in his pouch, poor Wallet was a sorry sight. His white feathers were streaked with oil and the sharp edge of a can had cut his beak. But he kept on working.

Feeling very weak and ill, Wallet fluttered down behind the sand dune and looked at the pile of tins. Though he had worked so hard, there was still only a very small pile of rubbish, and the lake seemed as dirty as ever. While he rested there, he suddenly noticed something moving. A man was coming towards him.

Wallet tried to fly away, but he was so tired that he just flopped down on the hot sand. The man came up to him. He was an old man, and wore shabby clothes and a large straw hat that shaded his face. "Well, now," said the man. "What have we here? A pelican, eh?"

The man turned the rubbish over with his foot. Then he picked up a scrap of dirty paper. If Wallet had been human, he would have known it was an envelope. The man read the address on the envelope and shook his head. He was very angry.

Then he walked away and packed up his things. He had been painting in the desert. His easel and paints and brushes went onto the back seat of his Landrover, and then he carefully picked up the exhausted Wallet and put him in beside them. He got in and drove away. He seemed to know where Wallet's lake was, and a short while later they were there.

The old man opened the door and let Wallet out. "You go and rest now," he said. "I'll be back, and I promise that your lake will be clean again soon." Wallet crept into his nest and fell asleep at once. It was all very strange.

A rumbling sound just like the one he had heard a week before woke him up. He raised his head above the reeds. A large black car had arrived. The driver jumped out and opened the back door. Out stepped the old man, but this time he wore a smart suit and a black hat.

Other men got out of the car too. They looked very sheepish and ashamed. The old man pointed at them and then at the lake. His voice was very angry. The men shuffled their feet in the sand and fanned their faces with their hats. After a while, they all drove away again. Wallet was very puzzled.

The next day a large truck arrived. Men climbed out and started clearing up the rubbish and loading it into the truck. The old man was also there in his black car, and he stayed with them until they had taken away every tin and every scrap of litter.

When they had gone, Wallet left his nest and went to investigate. All the rubbish had gone. Instead, there on the bank was a large, fresh fish the old man had brought especially for him. Wallet was delighted and gulped it down. The lake sparkled and shone in the sun. It was good to have a clean home to live in again.

Wallet flew round his lake for sheer pleasure, and as he flew he made up another little song:

"Wallet's lake,
Wallet's dunes,
Lucky, happy Wallet!"

DID YOU KNOW?

The *pelican* is a stout bird which takes off from the ground in a manner rather like a heavy transport plane! But once in the air, pelicans appear to fly for the sheer joy of flying. They use the hot air currents (called "thermals") to help them rise through the air in great sweeping circles before they glide slowly down again.

They usually feed as a flock, driving the fish into shallow water where they can be scooped up by the pelican's long bill and stored in the yellowish pouch underneath. You may have heard this rhyme:

A curious bird is the pelican;
Its beak holds more than its belly can!

But, in fact, it's the pouch not the beak which the pelican uses for storing the fish it catches.

Margaret von Tresckow

Waldi, the police dog

It was holiday time and the three sons of farmer Du Plessis had returned from boarding school at Heidelberg. This was the nearest town to their farm.

The boys – Peter, twelve, Charles, ten, and Johnny, just seven years old – were feeling full of mischief.

They were sitting on the stoep of the farm house, thinking hard what they could do on this beautiful summer day.

"Let's take the ball and practise football," suggested Peter, but his younger brothers shook their heads.

"Let's first go and buy sweets," said Johnny. "I've still got ten cents. How much have you got, Peter?"

Peter emptied his pocket and out came eight cents.

"Is that all? That's only eighteen cents. Never mind, let's see what Mrs Brown will give us."

Off they went, to the nearby trading store that sold everything from a pair of boots to a bag of mealie meal – and, of course, such treasures as sweets.

"Good morning to you," said Mrs Brown, the shopkeeper. "What will it be this time?"

The boys stood in front of the glass jars containing multi-coloured sweets. They certainly looked mouth-watering.

"Give us eighteen cents' worth of mixed sweets," said Charles.

"You won't get much for eighteen cents," said Mrs Brown, reaching for a small paper bag which she filled from one of the jars.

She went to the scales and weighed the bag. "Too much, this is actually twenty cents, but I'll let it go. Anything to please a good customer. Say hello to your ma for me," she added, handing the bag to Charles.

In no time the sweets had been shared equally and had disappeared into three different trouser pockets.

On the way home, the boys passed the police station. Outside, on the steps, was Police Sergeant Coetzee speaking to a farmer. The farmer, a big hefty fellow, was obviously annoyed.

"I wish you police would do something. I've lost five sheep during the last fortnight. Every time I'm here, you promise you will catch the thief and nothing is being done."

The boys passed quickly. Sergeant Coetzee was a nice fellow, but he had little help. How could he be everywhere at once?

"What are we going to do now?" asked Johnny when they were back at the farm.

"I've got an idea," said Peter. "Let's play detective. We'll follow the clues and find the sheep thief. What do you think?"

"That's O.K. with me," said Charles and Johnny nodded in agreement.

"All right then, from now on I'll be Lieutenant Peter and you two are Sergeant Charles and Sergeant John." He looked at Waldi, the family dachshund, who was lazily stretching himself in the sun.

"We need a police dog. Come here, Waldi, from now on you are a police dog, understand?" Waldi wagged his tail in recognition of this great honour.

"Now, boys," said the newly appointed

Lieutenant Peter, "get your guns and a lead for the dog and report back to me."

"Ready?" he asked when his brothers returned. "Then let's go." Big toy guns stuck out of the holsters they were wearing, and they looked eagerly out from under enormous cowboy hats.

Off they marched through the fields with Waldi in front, pulling at his lead. They were entering a wood when the dog suddenly got excited. He had his nose to the ground, and yelped and pulled with all his strength.

"Ah," said Lieutenant Peter, "attention! Our dog has found something. That may just be the spoor of the thief. Let's go."

They were excited. What were they going to do if they had to face a big strong man? Surely the thief would not take them seriously.

Waldi, by now, was tearing at his lead. The boys, although they were running, could hardly keep up. On the other side of the wood they came to a newly ploughed field. Waldi was yelping with excitement. There, a few steps away, a hare jumped up and crisscrossed over the field. Bewildered, the "detectives" looked at each other.

"Waldi, stop it," shouted an angry Lieutenant Peter. "Shame on you! You aren't fit to be a police dog."

Waldi, realizing he was in disgrace, hid his tail between his legs and whimpered softly.

"We'd better get back into the wood," said Peter, leading the way into the trees. Waldi followed obediently, all the time sniffing the ground.

Deeper and deeper they went into the forest. Suddenly Waldi went mad with excitement. Round he went in such crazy circles that Charles, who was holding the lead, could hardly hold him. The dog sniffed hard at the ground and then dashed off, following the scent.

The boys could see clearly that the grass was trodden down. Somebody must have walked here. Who could it be?

Waldi gave a sharp little whine, hesitating. There was a slight trace of blood on the moss.

The boys stared at it in horror. At last Lieutenant Peter gathered his courage and tried to appear cool. "It seems quite obvious that a murder has taken place. There is no other explanation." Remembering that he was a police lieutenant, he added, "Now, all men alert and follow the dog."

Waldi, by now, was carefully picking his way through thick undergrowth and the "detectives" followed in single file. They had walked for about ten minutes when Waldi suddenly yelped and backed away. But only for a split second, then he jumped forward with such force that he tore the lead out of Charles's hand. He was barking madly and through the bush the boys could see him making for a big rock on which a grown man sat. Over the man's shoulder hung a sheep. Its throat had been cut and drops of blood trickled from the wound.

The man had obviously been taken by surprise. He jumped up onto the rock to avoid the threatening teeth. The dog attacked again and again, snapping at the bare feet of the man, who didn't have any weapon, not even a stick. He tried to kick at Waldi, but that only doubled the dog's fury. Like lightning he jumped back to avoid the kick, then attacked again furiously the next moment.

"Run, run as fast as you can," said Peter to Charles and Johnny, "and bring Sergeant Coetzee here. Quick, quick!" The boys raced away.

Peter watched anxiously. "I'm only a boy – not a police officer at all," he thought to himself. "What can I do to help Waldi?"

Was the dog strong enough to keep going? The fight seemed to make him more eager to get at the man and though he was a small dog, his teeth were sharp.

The thief tried to jump down from the rock and run away, but each time Waldi took such a vicious snap at his legs that he quickly pulled them back.

Would help arrive in time? Peter's heart was beating fast and the seconds seemed like hours. "Please, Sergeant Coetzee, come quickly and help brave little Waldi," he prayed silently.

This time Waldi had not retreated quickly enough and got a nasty kick on the nose. He howled in pain and backed away. The thief took his chance, jumped from the rock and tried to run away. But Waldi had recovered and rushed at him, snapping at his heels.

"Don't move!" A clear voice rang through the forest. It was Sergeant Coetzee, followed by two breathless little boys.

The thief did not even try to get away. "Take this devil away," he shouted, hopping from one leg to the other as Waldi tried to get in a good bite at him. Peter caught him and a growling little dachshund watched as the thief was marched off to the police station.

Three small detectives followed, and with them went Waldi, carrying his tail high.

"After all," said Peter, "if it hadn't been for Waldi, we couldn't have caught the thief." He turned to the dog. "Waldi, you're the best police dog in the world. You deserve a medal for outstanding bravery."

That evening a contented little dachshund lay in his basket chewing an enormous bone. He was a realist and far preferred it to a medal.

Juliet Marais Louw

Poodle-sitter

I'm not used
to small dogs,
to neat dogs,
to town dogs;

I'm used
to tall dogs,
to fleet dogs,
to brown dogs.

I'm used to snug dogs,
give-me-a-hug dogs,
tumble-on-the-rug dogs,
with little girls and boys.

I'm not used to lap dogs,
"Mind-dear-he'll-snap" dogs,
"Don't-disturb-my-nap" dogs,
when people make a noise.

I'd never met refined dogs,
daintily designed dogs,
dogs who murmur courteously,
"Won't you take a walk with me?
There's something that I want to see –
I can't go on my own."

And though I fling the portals wide
on bush and beach and mountainside,
she will not cross the Great Divide,
though tempted with a bone.

I'm used to dogs that run
joyously, with day begun,
out into the rain (or sun)
and do it all alone.

John Struthers

Ou Bles, the trek ox

Once upon a time there was an old trek ox called Bles. He lived on a farm with the other cattle: the milk cows, the beef cows and their calves, and the sheep. Ou Bles was the leader of the herd, and every day he would lead them out of the kraal to graze, and in the evenings he would lead them back again. All the cattle respected their leader with his long horns.

But Ou Bles was not a happy trek ox. He had been trained to work on the farm, and the tractor did all the work now. It pulled the plough and the harrow, the planter and the cultivator. It even pulled the trailer with its sacks of grain piled high, and all of these things the trek oxen used to do. And so Ou Bles would look sadly at the tractor working busily, and long for the good old days. His old master was gone too. He would have given Ou Bles something to do, just to keep him happy. The new master – the old farmer's son – never paid any attention to Ou Bles any more. All of his time and attention were given to the tractor now. So Ou Bles, even though he was the leader of the herd, was an old, lonely, forgotten, sad trek ox.

Imagine everyone's surprise when, one morning, Ou Bles woke up and tried to make a noise like a tractor! Then, instead of leading the herd out into the fields to graze, he led them all around the farmyard. First of all, he went to the petrol tanks and tried to fill himself up with fuel for the day. But the petrol burned his mouth, so he spat it out. Then he went to the big new plough and tried to hitch himself up to it, but the plough was much too heavy for one old trek ox. So he went to the harrow and started to pull it down the road. The farmhands chased after him and took it away. Then they tried to chase him too . . . although they were a little bit frightened because he was acting so strangely.

Yes, Ou Bles really upset the farmyard that morning! The chickens all forgot to lay their eggs, the pigs all forgot to eat their morning mash, and all the turkeys and ducks gathered around to watch the fun. The young farmer, of course, was very annoyed with Ou Bles.

"I'll have to get rid of him," he muttered as he went back to the tractor – which was needing some repairs.

From that time onwards, the poor old trek ox became more and more peculiar. He was always getting in everybody's way: he even wanted to fight with the tractor! And although, of course, he was trying to help, he only succeeded in interfering and in making everyone mad.

And then, one weekend, the tractor finally broke down. So all the farm work had to stop, and the young farmer had to wait until the shops opened again on Monday morning before he could buy the spare parts which he needed for repairs. But on Sunday afternoon – while everyone was having a nice rest, and a nap – a terrible thing happened. A strong wind came and picked up some coals from the outside boiler fire. It carried them to one of the haystacks beside the farm buildings and set it on fire.

Ou Bles, wandering about, saw it first. He galloped into the farmyard and bellowed so hard that the farmer and his family all woke up. Soon they were all running about madly, trying to put the terrible fire out. It came closer and closer to the stables and barns, and even the farm house was in danger of catching alight.

Then Ou Bles really came to the rescue! He picked up the young farmer with his big wide horns and threw him onto his back and went galloping down to the water hole, where there was an old oxcart with some water drums on top of it standing forgotten beside the road. And the farmer called all the workmen and they filled the drums with water and Ou Bles pulled the oxcart up the hill to the fire, and it was soon put out.

Everyone stood around, looking at the damage. Then the young farmer came to Ou Bles and put his arm up over his neck and said, "Ou Bles, I was going to sell you on the next cattle sale. And now you have saved all the farm buildings for me. I could never sell you now!"

So Ou Bles was given the very best paddock as his own to graze. And whenever he wanted to pull the oxcart, the farmer found something for him to do. He soon found out, too, that Ou Bles was really very useful to have around the farm.

And, of course, the cattle were all very proud to have such a famous leader as Ou Bles had become.

C E Birkill

Manny the canny baboon

Manny, the old baboon, was sitting under a tree in our famous Kruger National Park. He was watching the cars drive slowly past. We kept the windows of our car shut as we drove towards him. Manny was sucking an orange which someone must have given him, even though that is not allowed.

He looked at our car with great interest. This was his chance. Why should he sit there alone, being stared at by everyone passing by? No! He would take a ride and see what was happening further down the road.

So we all had the surprise of our lives when a great grey hairy baboon landed on the bonnet of our car. It was Manny! And the car bonnet was hot. He danced about, rubbing his feet, and eventually sat down right in front of Father, who was driving. Dodge – dodge! Father had to peer past Manny to see where the car was going. Manny just sat there enjoying the scenery and looking at all the animals as the car crept slowly along. He was as curious as a tourist who has never been in a game reserve before.

For some distance he sat quite still, while we all watched him through the front windscreen. Then the cars coming the other way seemed to make him restless. He shifted about and then suddenly jumped across onto the bonnet of another car as it came past. That was how he would get back to the tree where he had joined us.

When we reached the camp, we were told that this was Manny's daily outing. That was why he was called "The Hitch-hiker".

Even baboons like a change of view at times!

DID YOU KNOW?

Baboons are dangerous! They are wild animals. However harmless they look, sitting by the side of the road, don't feed them and don't get out of your car. The more food they receive from cars, the more they will consider all cars as a source of food. Like any wild animal, baboons will fight to get food. Their usual menu includes wild fruit, roots, insects and lizards. Leave them with their natural food.

Raie Rodwell

No moss for Sammy

The bed of the Berg River is covered with thousands of stones smoothed by centuries of water washing over them. In summer they bask in the warm sun and in winter they huddle together in the icy water, dreaming of the lazy summer days ahead.

The Berg River stones had always been content with the pattern of their lives. The first signs of restlessness came from Sammy Stone, who shared a comfortable pool with his enormous family. He watched kingfishers darting among the willow trees, and dragonflies and frogs, until he could stand it no longer. He began to push on the sand in which he was embedded, but succeeded only in bumping against his Grandpa.

"What do you think you're doing?" grumbled Grandpa.

"I'm sick of always being in the same place," announced Sammy. "I want to see the rest of the world."

Grandpa was shocked. "I never thought that I'd hear grandchildren of mine talking like that. My family have been content to live here for generations."

"That's because they all lacked the spirit of adventure."

Grandpa snorted. "And how do you think you're going to leave home?"

"Just you wait and see."

"Before you do anything stupid, Sammy, remember that a rolling stone gathers no moss."

"Who wants moss, anyway? It's adventure I want," was Sammy's cocky reply.

"Don't be too smart, young man, you may regret it," advised Grandpa. And, as he said this, Grandpa thought with pleasure of the thick moss that helped to protect him against the iciness of winter. And the older he got, the more he was feeling the cold.

That night when the other stones were all asleep, Sammy forced himself to stay awake. As he expected, Mr and Mrs Otter came padding down to the pool to look for crabs. Sammy watched them slipping into the pool and called out, "Mr Otter, if you come over here, you'll find a fat crab."

Immediately the hungry otter scrambled over the stones towards Sammy.

"Hiding between my Grandpa and me is the juiciest crab I've ever seen. Just move me a bit if you want to catch him."

Mr Otter grabbed Sammy with his strong claws and pushed and pushed until – hey presto! – he was loose.

Rolling out of the pool, Sammy called out, "Oh, dear, that crafty crab has got away."

He rolled downstream until he felt tired and rested in a large pool. He was surprised to see clusters of reed cormorants on the banks, and realized that they were after the pretty spotted trout.

Thank goodness, thought Sammy, I'm not a trout. Wait till Grandpa hears about this. Then, suddenly, it struck him that perhaps he would never see his family again. It was easy going downstream, but how would he get upstream? Oh, well, he would face that problem later. In the mean time, he was going to seek adventure.

At that moment he felt something heavy

on him. It was a man in rubber boots who was stepping across the river. He was carrying a bag on his back and holding a fishing rod. Oh, no, thought Sammy, not another enemy for those poor little fishes. Sammy wanted to move on, but decided to protect the trout hiding below him until the man had gone, before he travelled on.

It wasn't much later that Sammy found himself in danger. Two men came along in a canoe, rowing furiously. One of the oars hit Sammy hard on his back. "Gosh," said Sammy, "that was sore." To his surprise one of the trout came and rubbed softly against him where he had been hit.

"Thanks," said Sammy, "that makes my back feel much better."

"You protected my family," said the trout, "and it's my pleasure to repay you for your kindness. I'd move on quickly, if I were you," went on the trout, "soon there'll be lots of canoeists practising for the annual big race, and then we're all in danger."

Sammy thanked the trout and rolled off at

once. That night he rested under a bridge, and before long he heard dreadful noises and saw enormous shapes passing overhead. For the first time since leaving home he was frightened.

"Excuse me," he said timidly to the fat stone next to him, "but could you please tell me what those things are up there?"

The stone eyed him contemptuously. "Did you hear that, guys?" he said to the other stones. "This stranger doesn't know a car when he sees one."

"Well," said Sammy, feeling rather ashamed of his ignorance, "upstream in the valley where I come from, we don't see cars."

After a noisy night when he hardly slept, Sammy moved off early next morning. He went past sand-banks where martins, swallows and colourful bee-eaters flew.

Suddenly he noticed that the water tasted different, sort of salty, and he realized that he was nearing the sea. How exciting! Soon the river flowed between stretches of muddy water. Sammy saw flamingoes, avocets and herons wading among the reeds along the edge of the water. On and on he rolled, until ahead of him he saw a great blue stretch of water, and he knew that this was the sea and the end of his long journey.

Moving over the water was a large black shape. It wasn't a fish or an otter. Whatever could it be? At that moment a seagull came to rest next to Sammy.

"Excuse me, but could you please tell me what that is out there on the water?"

"That," said the gull, in a very superior tone of voice, "is the ship on which I have just travelled from Cape Town. So much easier than flying. And quicker too. I come here every year, at this time, because the fishing is so good."

Sammy looked around for a comfortable spot where he knew he would have to spend the rest of his life. His surface was rough and dirty, he was tired and sore, but he had enjoyed the journey. He thought of his family in their secluded pool, gathering moss and leading such placid lives.

Well, he didn't have any moss on him, and now that he was near the sea, maybe he never would have any. But he didn't care.

He had travelled a long way, seen the outside world and many new and wonderful things. And now he knew far more than any other member of his large family. He was sorry that he would never see them again. How he would have liked to go home to tell them about his adventures, and encourage them to travel, rather than be stick-in-the-muds for ever and ever! He was sure that even Grandpa would have enjoyed his tales. No, he would never regret having been a rolling stone.

DID YOU KNOW?

The *Berg River* is the most important river in the Western Cape. From its beginnings in the mountains around Franschhoek, it flows north and west for nearly 330 kilometres until it reaches the sea at St Helena Bay. Its mouth at Velddrif is large enough for ocean-going fishing-boats to sail in and offload their catches in shelter.

Explorers in the days of Jan van Riebeeck followed its banks to find their way north. The old town of Paarl stretches along eleven kilometres of the Berg River. The Voëlvlei Dam supplies water to Malmesbury, Darling and as far south as Tygerberg. The Berg River also supplies Saldanha Bay with fresh water.

Every year since 1962, the Berg River Marathon has taken place – when canoes make the four-day journey from Paarl to Velddrif.

Juliet Marais Louw

When Jannie kept house

When Jannie's mother went to hospital, she was very worried about what would happen to Jannie and his father in her absence.

"Who will keep house?" she demanded. "Who on earth will do the cooking?"

"I will," said Jannie.

So Jannie's father took her to hospital in the car. Jannie came home from school to an empty house – no one in the kitchen, no one in the bedroom. But the refrigerator was full of things that just needed warming up. For some days the cooking was easy. There was no need to buy anything except bread.

Then suddenly the fridge was bare – like Mother Hubbard's cupboard.

"We'll boil eggs," said Jannie.

That was fine. Jannie knew exactly how to boil eggs. He bought a dozen at the supermarket, and he boiled eggs and boiled eggs for every meal. He also put bread, margarine and jam on the table and they ate eggs, bread, margarine and jam for days and days.

One morning Dad said, "Jannie, I cannot eat another egg. I seem to dream of eggs all day and I think I am beginning to look like an egg. So do you. In fact, you look so like an egg I can hardly tell the difference."

When Dad had gone off to work, Jannie looked at himself anxiously in the mirror. He was relieved to see that he could still tell the difference between himself and the egg he had had for breakfast. However, he saw his father's point, so that afternoon when he came home from school he went over to Mrs Joubert, who lived next door to them in the little curved street called Marina Avenue, and he said, "Please, Mrs Joubert, how do you make stew?"

"I'll make you a stew, Jannie," began Mrs Joubert, but Jannie broke in very decidedly, "Oh no, thank you, I want to make it myself."

"All right then," said Mrs Joubert. "You cut the meat into little bits. Then you turn them in flour and fry them brown in oil and add a little water and salt and vegetables. Then you put on the lid and boil it slowly for a long time."

That sounded easy. He took some money out of the tin in the kitchen cupboard where Mother had left it in case he had to buy something during the day when Dad was at work. He ran to the supermarket and bought a packet of stewing-steak, which was what Mrs Joubert had suggested. He did exactly what she had told him, and after about two hours the steak looked just like a stew and he was so proud that he could not wait for Dad to come home and admire him. So he went next-door to call Mrs Joubert.

"Do please come and look at my stew," he pleaded.

"Of course I will," said Mrs Joubert, who was the nicest possible person.

When she lifted the lid, she exclaimed, "Why, Jannie, that looks and smells just perfect. I think you should have some rice with that and then it will be a lovely meal."

The rice was in a container on the top shelf. It was a big container. Jannie liked rice, so he poured the whole lot into the stew and sat down at the kitchen table to do

his homework. After a while he saw the lid of the pot lift off and to his surprise it was being lifted up by rice. This was something he had not expected at all. He took another pot and scooped the top layer of rice off into it. But the rice grew and grew. He filled all the pots in the kitchen. More and more rice bulged over the edge of the pot. Jannie perspired and filled the milk jug and put more water in the pot and when that was full, he went next door to Mrs Bosman who lived on the other side of Mrs Joubert, because he felt he had bothered Mrs Joubert enough for one afternoon. Mrs Bosman gladly lent him a pot. When that was full, he crossed the street to Mrs Thomas. The whole kitchen table was covered with pots of rice.

Dad came home.

"Well, I'm blessed!" he exclaimed.

They sat down to supper and ate rice. Now and then, in amongst it, they came upon a shred of meat or tomato-skin or carrot to recall the fact that it had started off as a stew. Jannie's father ate and laughed and laughed and ate and when he had had enough, he and Jannie began to carry round pots of rice to the neighbours. The whole of Marina Avenue had rice for supper that night.

"You told me to have rice with it," said Jannie reproachfully to Mrs Joubert when he brought her her share.

"Yes, but I meant you to cook it in a separate pot, and only a little – a quarter of a cup would be more than enough for the two of you."

Well, how was Jannie to know that? Anyway, next evening he made another stew and this time he cooked a quarter of a cup of rice in another pot and it was a very good meal.

In any case his mother came home soon after this and then all his troubles were over.

Barbara Campbell-Tait

Groot Constantia

The lady named Constantia,
she wears vine leaves in her hair.
There's all about her great big house
a creepy, creepy air.

"Come in," she smiles, "and look around,"
but sit we do not dare,
For ghostly hands have deftly slung
a cord around each chair.

The portraits eye us slyly
as we tip-toe 'cross the floor.
I *know* a *skelm's* hiding there
behind the bedroom door!

A *spooksel* in the ginger jar
pops up the lid to peer.
Around the copper pots
the *tokoloshes* leap and leer.

A monster treads the *brandsolder* –
I see the ceiling shake!
Let's dash into the garden
and grab a garden-rake!

The janitor comes jangling keys,
"It's nearly five o'clock."
We hear him mutt'ring to himself,
"I have the wine to lock."

For Ganymede astride his swan
above the cellar door,
With half a chance would love to roll
those barrels on the floor.

But listen! from the slave quarters,
"Woo-oo!" – an eerie wail.
Come, come, my good companions,
it is time we all turned tail!

The clatter of a carriage as
we hurry down the drive,
Can only mean that Simon van der Stel
has come alive!

DID YOU KNOW?

Groot Constantia was the home of Simon van der Stel, an early governor of the Cape. Simonstown and Stellenbosch are both named after him. It is a beautiful house but, sadly, the one you visit now is not the original. That burned down in 1925, but it was rebuilt as accurately as possible and now contains a wonderful collection of old Cape furniture, paintings and china.

A double row of oak trees leads from the house to an ornamental pool which was once used for bathing. It is said that you might meet an elderly man, wrapped up in towels, walking back from his bath. If you do, greet him politely, for he is the ghost of Simon van der Stel.

Joy Hopking

Bushy's adventure

Bushy was a bushbaby. He and his mother lived with other bushbabies in a fig tree forest in a game reserve in Zululand.

Bushy was very small and very fluffy, and he could hardly be seen as he clung tightly to his mother's furry tummy. He loved it when she jumped from branch to branch because it felt like flying. But when she walked along the branches looking for insects, Bushy would poke his head out of her fur and then you could see his pointy nose and his big bright eyes. His mother gave him juicy caterpillars to eat, and also ripe berries when she could find them.

Sometimes at night Bushy's mother and the other bushbabies would leave the forest and hop, skip and jump across the grass to a mealie field. Bushy and the other little ones clung tightly to their mothers as they hunted for locusts and insects amongst the corn.

When Bushy was big enough to leave his mother he loved to play in the mealie field. The mealie stalks were just the right size for his little hands to grasp, and he used to practise climbing them and jumping across to the next mealie plant.

One night when his mother was busy eating, he felt very adventurous as he climbed and jumped amongst the stalks. Suddenly he found himself at the edge of the mealie field with open veld in front of him. He looked around, but he could not see his mother or any of the other bushbabies, though he could hear the crying noise they made as they called to each other. Feeling very brave, he jumped out onto the cool grass. He had never played on grass outside the forest before and he thought it was great fun to dance about in the moonlight. He found some ants and carefully picked them up and chewed them. They were peppery, but Bushy liked the taste.

The moonlight was fading and soon the sun would be rising. As the light grew brighter Bushy began to feel sleepy. He hopped slowly towards a shady tree. At its foot he settled down with his big bushy tail curled around his furry little body. He was soon sound asleep.

Meanwhile all the other bushbabies had had enough to eat. Suddenly they heard a man shouting. The farmer who owned the mealie field was very cross when he found that many of his mealies had been broken. The frightened bushbabies scampered back to the forest, climbed quickly into the highest branches, and soon all was quiet because the bushbabies were sound asleep. They always slept in the daytime and woke up in the evening just before it got dark.

The only one who was not sleeping was Bushy's poor mother, who was very worried about her naughty little child.

Now, Bushy had been sleeping at the foot of the tree for quite a long time, and he woke to the sound of voices. In a fright he sprang up and tried to climb the tree, but he was too frightened to go very high. So he kept quite still as two children came towards him.

"Look at this little animal," said the boy, whose name was Barry. He sounded so

friendly that Bushy was not afraid when Barry picked him up.

"It's a bushbaby," said Barry's sister, Claire. "They usually sleep in the daytime because they don't like sunlight."

Barry wondered how he could shelter the little creature from the light. "I know," he said, "I'll put him into my shirt pocket."

Bushy was small enough to fit in, and he curled up comfortably, but the tip of his fluffy tail stuck out of the pocket and tickled Barry's neck.

The children lived in a house on the edge of the game reserve where their father was a game ranger. They hurried home to show Bushy to him. Barry asked if he could keep Bushy as a pet, but his father knew that wild animals are always happiest living in their natural surroundings. So he said that it would be kinder to find Bushy's mother and then take him back to her.

Late in the afternoon, when the shadows were growing long and the air had the cool feeling of approaching night, Bushy awoke. "Where am I?" he wondered as he sleepily opened his eyes and peered over the edge of the box where Barry had made him comfortable with one of Claire's dolls' blankets. Bushy raised one soft round ear, then the other. Then he flattened his ears again because there was no sound around him. He stretched one arm slowly over the edge of the box and clambered out onto a big wooden shelf. It was the kitchen dresser.

At that moment Barry came in. "Hello,

Bushy," he said, "you have had a long sleep. Are you hungry?" He was just about to pick him up, when *Spring!* Bushy leapt onto his shoulder. Then, *Spring!* Bushy jumped again, this time onto the top of the dresser. *Spring! Spring!* He jumped and jumped, all over the kitchen.

"Bushy," said Barry, laughing, "come down here and have some supper."

By this time Bushy was sitting on the pelmet above the window. He could smell the cool evening air, and he thought about juicy flying ants and he felt very hungry.

He tried to climb down from the pelmet, but his little arms could not reach the window, so he jumped down onto the back of the kitchen chair.

Barry thought, I hope Bushy does not disappear into the night, because he really will be lost then. So he made a grab and caught Bushy on the chair.

"You rascal," he laughed, as he hugged him gently, "you gave me quite a fright. Now let's see what Father suggests for your supper."

Barry's father said that bushbabies liked insects and fruit. There were grapes in the fridge, but where could they find suitable insects?

At that moment his mother, who was busy gardening, called, "Come and look at the roses." There were big fat green grasshoppers sitting on the leaves, eating them as fast as they could.

"Well," said his father, "that's lovely!"

"I don't think they're lovely," said his mother indignantly. "They're eating my best roses."

Father laughed and called, "Look, Barry! Mother has found lots of food for Bushy." He picked up a plump grasshopper and gave it to the little animal, who was sitting on Barry's shoulder.

Bushy looked at it with his head on one side and his ears going up and down, then he politely took it in his tiny little fingers. Suddenly he realized that it was good to eat, and crunch, crunch, crunch, he gobbled it up.

He sat on Barry's shoulder and ate five grasshoppers one after another, as Barry walked among the roses picking them off and offering them to his little friend.

Eventually Bushy had had enough, and when he was offered another he turned his head away. It was nearly dark, so Barry took him indoors and told Claire about the grasshoppers.

"Ugh!" she said. "I'm glad I didn't see him crunching them up. Look, there's a grasshopper's leg stuck to your shirt."

Barry brushed it off, and Claire handed Bushy a grape. Bushy had never seen a grape because they don't grow in the forest. So he would not touch it until Claire broke it in half and he saw how juicy it was. Then he enjoyed several, carefully licking up all the juice that had spilt on Barry's jersey.

They offered him water, but he did not want any. Barry's father said that he had probably had enough to drink from the juice of the grapes.

Now that his meal was over, Bushy became very lively. While the family was having supper, he jumped around the room; from the chairs onto the mantelpiece, then onto the picture frames, and up onto the picture rail. He had a wonderful time, but Mother held her breath in case he broke a vase on the mantelpiece or knocked down a picture. She need not have worried, because Bushy was very light and did not damage anything. Bushbabies keep their feet damp so that they can cling onto things and not fall; but he left little wet footmarks on the white paint, which Mother did not like at all.

When it was time for Barry and Claire to go to bed, Barry caught Bushy and put him on the floor. "Come along, Bushy," he said, walking away.

Bushy jumped along the floor, following Barry down the passage to the bedroom. At the door Barry stopped. In a moment Bushy had leapt up to Barry's waist; then, climbing up his back, he sat on his shoulder.

Suddenly Bushy felt very happy, because he thought he saw his mother's fur. But it was Barry's hair that he nestled into, clinging tightly to Barry's head.

Barry yelled with surprise. Claire looked into the bedroom, and then she laughed and laughed.

Mother and Father came in to see what all the noise was about. When they saw Bushy sitting so snugly in Barry's hair, they laughed too.

"Take him out," pleaded Barry. "How can I go to bed with a bushbaby in my hair?"

Father carefully took him off Barry's head and said, "He can spend the night in the aviary, where there is plenty of room for him to jump about."

So Bushy had a wonderful time in the large bird-cage, running along the perches and jumping from one to another all night. The budgies did not know what the strange creature was, but he did not hurt them.

In the morning Father went for a walk on the edge of the forest where the mealie field was, and there he met the farmer. Father asked him if he knew where the bushbabies lived. Together they walked into the forest and looked up into the trees. Soon the farmer pointed to a dark bundle on a high branch, and then another and another, and whispered to Father that this looked like the bushbabies' daytime resting place. They decided not to disturb them and went quietly away.

Father went home and told Barry that he had found the bushbabies. So that evening, after Bushy had slept all day in his box in the kitchen, they took him to the forest. They soon saw bright eyes shining down at them from amongst the leaves and then – Oh, happiness! Bushy recognised his mother sitting sadly on a branch. He gave Barry's cheek a quick lick to say goodbye.

Barry understood, and put him into his father's hands. Bushy was lifted onto a high branch, and as he scrambled along it his mother saw him. She came bounding over to him, all fear of the strangers on the ground forgotten in her excitement at seeing her lost baby again.

The last his friends saw of him was a little furry ball disappearing into the fur of the big furry mother bushbaby.

"Goodbye, Bushy," said Barry, a little sadly.

Bushy told his mother and all his friends about his adventures with Barry and his family. Everyone was so interested that they forgot to play in the mealie field that night. But Bushy's mother scolded him and warned him not to wander away from her again because not all humans were as kind as Barry and his family. Bushy snuggled up to her and promised to try to be good in future.

DID YOU KNOW?

The *bushbaby* is a delightful, cuddly-looking member of the monkey family. He looks like a small koala bear with a long bushy tail. The ones in this story live in the wooded parts of Zululand. Bushbabies are timid, gentle creatures but be careful of petting them as they can give a nasty bite if they are frightened. They make nests of leaves and grass in the branches of trees, and sleep during the daytime in family groups.

Jay Heale

The ring of the king

(An African fable retold)

Once there was a king – a king with a ring. That ring was the secret of his power and greatness.

The ring was made of gold brought up the River Nile, inlaid with silver brought up the River Congo, and topped with diamonds brought up the River Zambezi – though exactly where they came from, no one ever knew. This ring was so magical that whoever wore it was protected from all mortal danger. That meant that no matter how many people came charging round the corner waving spears and axes and shooting arrows, the king could never get hurt. Provided, of course, that he was wearing the ring.

So the king wore the ring all the time – giving judgement in his court, eating stupendous feasts which lasted all day, being carried on a special sort of bed covered with ostrich feathers through the streets of his city (for of course he never walked unless he had to) and even sleeping in the royal bedchamber surrounded by all his favourite wives at night.

(As you will have guessed, this is a story from long ago, when kings were allowed to collect many wives. But it isn't a habit that you should try to copy.)

The king wore the magic ring every hour of every day, except once a month when he went for his ceremonial bath. Even kings have to wash sometimes. If the weather was very hot, he sometimes washed as often as once a week. On these occasions, the king was carried to the crystal-clear pool beside the waterfall. There all his servants and his children and his many wives bowed low to him, and then backed away out of sight. A king does like to have his bath in peace.

Once they were safely gone, the king took off his crown of gold and ivory and peacock feathers, his cloak of gold and silk and precious stones, his sandals of ebony and rhinoceros hide, and his robe of the purest white linen. And then he took off his ring and hid it in a place so cunning and so secret that not even his servants, nor his children, nor even his many many wives could make the slightest guess where it was. Perhaps they tried to guess, but they were never right. And as soon as he had finished his royal bath, the ring was the first thing the king put on again, before he allowed anyone to come anywhere near. He treasured the ring, because it made him the most powerful king in Africa.

But the day came when he stepped, dripping, out of his ceremonial bath into the warming sun, to find that the ring was not there. At first with amazement and then with fear, the king searched his secret hiding place and all around it. The ring was gone. There was no chance of an accident. It must have been stolen. Somebody – somebody among all his servants and his children and the many many wives (whom you know about) must have found out the hiding place and dared to take the ring.

The king was furious. But he was also afraid. If he offered great rewards for the finding of the ring, then everyone would know that he no longer had it. They would know that he was no longer protected from harm. They would know that he was no longer the most powerful king in Africa.

So for days the king sat and worried. He paced up and down his palace, he sat for hours staring at the ground or at the sky, he couldn't sleep. All his wives shook their heads in sorrow, and his children kept well away. It was his favourite wife – the one with the red garnet necklaces – who persuaded him to tell her what was wrong.

She knew at once that the king had wasted too much time already. Straight away she went to the house of the wisest of all the diviners. Now, a diviner can be called by many titles: some call him a medicine-man, others call him a witchdoctor or a sorcerer. In different parts of Africa, he is thought of in different ways – as a worker of magic, as a healer, as a teller of the future. This particular diviner was all three and a bit more, and his name was Zafusa.

With wild eyes and jangling rings on his arms, Zafusa sprang into the house where the king sat. Plumes of feathers danced and waved in his head-dress, and strips of furry skin dangled from his waist. He looked like a feathered leopard with a hundred tails. He listened silently while the king explained about the stolen ring. Then Zafusa opened one of the leather pouches that hung from his beadwork belt, and took out the set of bones that he used to find the answers to hard questions. Smoothing out a circle in the sand, Zafusa held the bones towards the sky, gave a sharp cry and then dropped the bones. Carefully, he examined the pattern in which they lay. Then – while the king held his breath just as much as you are doing – Zafusa straightened up and looked at him.

"Your ring will be found, Your Majesty," he said. "The thief is close to us."

"Who is it?" demanded the king.

Zafusa shook his head. "You shall see. It will not need magic. Send for your builders and woodcutters."

The king did so at once, and Zafusa explained to them what was needed. At dawn on the next day, everyone who could possibly have had any chance to steal the ring was gathered together in the great square in front of the king's front door. It was an impressive front door too, with a tall flight of steps and mysterious carvings all round the doorway.

The king appeared at the top of the steps and stood there, staring silently at the bowing people. Then he clapped his hands and soldiers suddenly appeared all round the square, ready armed with sharpened spears so no one could escape. Through a small archway appeared Zafusa, all the more terrible now with white circles around each eye and strange dark designs on his body. Following him came the woodcutters with great numbers of straight wooden rods – the kind of sticks used for making huts. They heaped the sticks in the centre of the square.

Zafusa danced around the sticks, chanting in a language nobody had heard before, and it was clear to even the smallest child that he was casting a spell on the sticks. Then, at the king's command, everyone in the square was given one stick.

"Take care!" thundered Zafusa. "These sticks are full of power. Do not lose them. Have them with you all through today. Bring them back here at dawn tomorrow. As the sun rises, we shall see what we shall see."

Sticks of power! All the people were amazed. The sticks looked so ordinary. They compared sticks with one another. They all looked just the same. A few were a little thicker or thinner, but they were all the same length. In fact, they were all *exactly* the same length. Curious!

The guards moved, and the servants, children and wives were allowed to leave. They

went backwards, of course, for no one ever turned a back on the king. So they all saw the king beckoning with his finger to his favourite wife, the one with the red garnet necklaces.

As she knelt before him, he whispered in her ear, "The thief is as good as caught. The stick will catch him. The stick of the thief will grow by the thickness of three fingers. But don't tell anyone I said so."

And as the king strode inside his carved doorway, all the wives, children and servants crowded round the one with the red garnet necklaces to find out what the king had said. Now the wife was a careful woman. She never said a thing to anyone, except just to her own extra-special friend. That friend was a trustworthy woman too, and she only told her mother and her wise old aunt. But the strange thing was that by the time the sun set that evening, every single person who had been in the square knew that by dawn the thief's stick would have grown in length by the thickness of three fingers.

Night came as swiftly and silently as it always did – because that was something that this king gave strict orders about – and there were a lot of very excited people when the first touches of dawn showed that the night was over. Everyone gathered in the square and everyone had his stick, which was an absolute wonder, for one small boy always seemed to lose everything.

The sun slid up into the sky, and suddenly – there was Zafusa, a gleaming spear in his hand, glaring at the people. The king appeared, carried on his special travelling bed with the ostrich feathers. (All the excitement had left his legs quite weak.) Beside him walked the Chief Builder in the kingdom, with his measuring rod.

Stick after stick was measured, all the way round the square. Not one of them had grown so much as a finger-nail in length. But there was *one* stick, carried by a fat sweating servant with a shifty look in his eyes, that was exactly the thickness of three fingers *shorter* than everyone else's.

"There's the thief!" shrieked Zafusa, leaping high into the air and waving his spear.

"Take him!" yelled the king, ordering the royal guards into action. "Feed him to the lions!"

And the silly servant forgot that the ring protected him and fell on his knees and cried and blubbered and took off the ring from the hand he had been hiding and gave it to the king and cried some more and begged for mercy. And the king was so pleased to have his ring back and be the most powerful king in Africa once again that he allowed the royal lions to go without their breakfast.

The thief was set free. Free, that is, apart from a small punishment, because you can't do things like that and expect to get off completely. He had to run three times round the city, and the children chased him all the way round all three times, and they found *quite* a different use for their sticks.

"How did you manage that?" asked the king, as he was recovering in his private chamber, and Zafusa stood watching bag after bag of gold being brought from the king's treasury. "Your magic must be even stronger than the magic of the ring."

"Not so," said Zafusa. "I told you it would not need magic. All it needed was one very guilty man. He knew so well that he was the thief that he really believed his stick *had* grown by three fingers during the night. So he took a saw and cut off that amount and thought no one would notice."

He tied up the bags of gold in a spare sheepskin he had thoughtfully brought with him and bowed once to the king.

"There is more than one kind of magic, Your Majesty!"

Penny Rivett-Carnac

Mr Fataar's fantastic fruit lorry

Between the mountain and the sea
where the South-East wind blows gustily
greengrocers' trucks go trundling by
with fruit and vegetables heaped high;
stopping at houses, giving a hoot,
as if to say, "Come buy my fruit!"

Well, the lorry that visited Tahira Mahout
is the one I want to tell you about.
It had magical powers –
no, don't shake your head!
I know that's what Tahira said.
Just listen carefully and I'll tell you
how she discovered what it could do!

Every Friday after tea
Tahira would wait eagerly
for the lorry to call at her front gate –
around four o'clock – it was never late.
It was painted blue. You could see from far
the name of the owner – M. FATAAR.

And the back of the lorry was just like a shop
– sacks and boxes right up to the top!
Apples, bananas, cauliflowers, grapes.
A jumble of colours, a jumble of shapes!
Mr Fataar was the jolliest chap.
Both winter and summer he wore a blue cap.
(Though Tahira found it very queer
that he kept a pencil behind his ear.)

His nephew, Dickie, a lad of ten,
helped him fetch and weigh out the fruit,
and then
he'd carry the heavy basket right in
to your kitchen, and he'd give you a grin!

Each week he was paid a small amount
for helping his uncle to carry and count.
"I'm saving it all," he told folk with pride.
(His dream was a brand-new bike to ride!)
He kept this money in a purse made of leather
in a shiny tin box, where it stayed, together
with all the cash Mr Fataar made.
And now comes the dreadful part, I'm afraid:

One fateful Friday this same tin box
was left in the cab with its key in the lock,
and worse, the door was left standing ajar!
While Tahira's mother and Mr Fataar,
round by the gate, were chatting together
(the price of fruit, I suppose, or the weather)
and Dickie was carrying the basket inside,
only Tahira was watching –
and Tahira spied
a tall thin man in a navy-blue sweater
creep into the cab! She felt so upset, her
voice wouldn't work!
Then she managed to squeak
and raise the alarm, even though she felt weak.
"Help, Dickie, quick! There's a thief in the cab!"
But already the thief had managed to grab
the precious tin box. It was all so well-timed –
down the road raced a scooter,
and he jumped on behind!

"Come on! After him!" yelled Mr Fataar,
"I'll chase those crooks, no matter how far!"
He leapt to his seat; the engine spluttered;
and bumping about in the back, all cluttered
with fruit and vegetables of every shape,
were Dick and Tahira!
"That crook shan't escape!"

The thieves had a start,
  but the lorry went fast
and they almost caught up
  with the scooter at last,
but it dodged between cars
  and took corners quite blind
as they raced and they chased,
  leaving Wynberg behind.

Then, just at the church,
  the rogues were in sight,
held up on Carr Hill
  by the robot's red light.
The lorry roared up –
  luck was not with them then
for, as soon as they got there,
  the lights changed again!
Down the hill raced those crooks,
  straight for the Main Road.
"That's the worst place for us
  with our heavy load,"
groaned Dickie, "gee, a big lorry like this
will get caught in the traffic!
  We should give it a miss!"

So, desperate to stop them,
  or make them change course,
Dick grabbed a ripe orange
  and threw it with force.

It sailed through the air
  and came down with a splat
straight onto the thin crook's
  brown woollen hat!
He yelled, and nearly fell right off his seat –
but the scooter sped on to
  that traffic-filled street.
And though Mr Fataar pressed hard
  on the hooter
nobody realised there were thieves
  on that scooter!

Just as Dickie had feared,
  very soon they were stuck
with the scooter ahead,
  caught behind a large truck.
And then came a stroke of incredible luck!
Glancing down, Mr Fataar saw there,
  at his feet,
a note bearing plans for the robbers to meet
that the thief must have dropped
  as he made his escape.
And what he read out
  made the fruit vendor gape –
"Proceed with the cash to the boat *Daisy May,*
which you'll find lying berthed
  in the harbour, Kalk Bay."
"We'll catch them yet, children," he yelled,
  "don't despair!

They're off to Kalk Bay,
  but we'll beat them there!"

Off they set once again with much haste
  and such speed
down that busy main road,
  they forgot to take heed,
and a traffic cop, parked behind a large oak,
said, "Something must surely be up
  with that bloke!"
For the lorry was really a very strange sight
as it sped, dropping fruit to the left
  and the right.
So, to add to their woes,
  was this traffic cop, trailing
behind on his bike
  and his siren was wailing!

But ahead the blue sea was already in view.
"We cannot stop now;
  there's just one thing to do –
we must first catch the thieves,
  and then we'll explain!"
said Mr Fataar. "They won't feel
  we're to blame!"
And just at that moment
  the scooter they spied
turning left through the gates
  to the harbour inside,
where the fishing boats floated
  and bobbed on the tide.
"We've got them at last –
  they'll be trapped!" Dickie cried.
But he'd quite forgotten,
  there remained one big snag –
and that was the man with his little red flag
who stood at the gates
  when a train rattled past.
And now one was coming,
  and coming quite fast!
There was nothing for it –
  they just had to stop;
and behind them, of course,
  was that same traffic cop!

The train snorted by;
  the red flag waved them through;
they raced for the quayside,
  for already they knew
that those thieves would have jumped
  on the boat *Daisy May*.
Sure enough, there she was!
  And just sailing away.

They had failed;
  and they gazed with despair in each heart.
But, don't fear, we have reached
  the most wonderful part –

that amazing fruit lorry
now took matters in hand.
It drove straight off the quayside!
And, as if on command,
its four rubber tyres began to expand.
When its wheels hit the water,
it started to float!
It had changed itself into a fruit-lorry-boat!
The traffic cop stared –
he thought he'd gone daft.
First there was a blue lorry,
next a blue hover-craft!
And as for those thieves –
they were so filled with fear
when they saw, o'er the sea,
the fruit lorry appear,
that they jumped overboard –
right into the waves –
and they would have been washed
to their watery graves
if soft-hearted Tahira hadn't started to cry,
"How can we just turn back
and leave them to die?"

(They were choking and splashing
and gasping for air!)
Then Mr Fataar had a clever idea.
"Let's sew all these sacks
in a sort of a net
then we'll use that to haul those two
out of the wet!"

So they joined orange bags up
with pieces of string,
threw them into the sea
with an almighty fling,
and managed to scoop up
those two drowning men
and drag them aboard the fruit lorry;
and then,
when they saw what they'd caught,
they shouted with glee –
it was not just the thieves
they'd pulled out of the sea
but a very fine haul of silvery snoek!
"Now to tie up our catch!"
and they roped up each crook!

Well, the boat *Daisy May* was left,
drifting around,
so Dick leapt aboard,
and guess what he found –
that shiny tin box, sitting all safe and sound
in the cabin below. And that isn't all –
when they'd tied the boat up
to the grey harbour wall,
they found it was full of valuable booty!

Now the traffic cop,
all in the course of his duty,
had called the police,
who were pleased with this hoard,
so they gave Mr Fataar a great big reward.

Nowadays, on a Friday, to Tahira's delight,
when the fruit lorry calls,
it's a wonderful sight.
In paint new and shiny,
and in black letters bold
on its side you'll see written,
BOTH FRUIT AND FISH SOLD.
And Dickie has bought the smartest of bikes
(Which Tahira can ride whenever she likes.)

So you see why Tahira loves telling the story
of the magical lorry and its moment of glory.

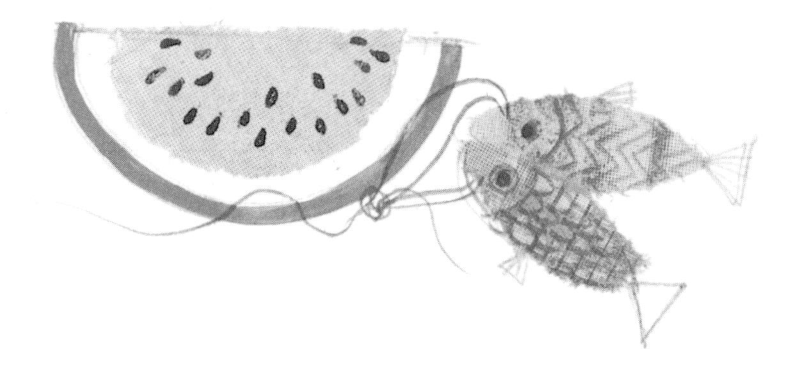

Helen Fawkes

A little Karoo story

Once upon a short time ago, in one particular house, in one particularly sunny South African valley, lived Johnbo' van Zyl. He was a boy of about your age, or maybe two months younger, who was blessed with the wonderful knack of running into magical things, in places where you would really and truly least expect to find magical things.

Take, for example, his grandfather's attic.

When Johnbo' first peeped into the attic through the door in the ceiling, his nose became suddenly very, very itchy – the "magic-in-the-air" itch, not the "cold-in-the-nose" kind – and he knew he just had to investigate further.

He raced outside and along the well-worn path to the kraal where the farm-workers lived, shaking dewdrops from the trees as he ran, and looking for all the world like a tiny thunder-storm moving with great haste through the Karoo morning.

He found his friend, Sunday, stirring a huge pot of mealies, which he was probably cooking for breakfast, since it was that time of the day.

"Sunday," said Johnbo', "come quickly, I smell ma-a-agic in the air," and he did a little African dance because he was pretending to be a witchdoctor, or something equally powerful.

Sunday waved his stirrer in the air and joined in the dance in a frenzied whirl of mealie-porridge.

While they dance, let me quickly explain about Sunday – no, that's not his real name, as you were probably wondering. His real name is long and full of clicks and means "Oh-little-black-shiny-one-born-on-a-Sunday-afternoon", but for obvious reasons he came to be known as just "Sunday".

Their frenzied dance was soon put to a stop, as Sunday's mother closed in like a big, black thunder-cloud, and sent the two boys flying down the path to the farmhouse, their bottoms stinging from the hard end of the stirrer.

The attic was cold after the warmth of the morning, and both boys shivered slightly with chilly excitement as they crept through the door in the ceiling. Their candles sent shadows and spiders scuttling over the attic walls.

"Sunday," said Johnbo', "do you feel the ma-a-a-gic?"

"I fe-e-e-l it," said Sunday, and the boys started searching furiously for it.

After about half an hour, which felt like two minutes because time goes very fast when you are searching furiously, Johnbo' lifted a pile of old riding-boots and discovered, to his utmost delight, exactly what they had been looking for.

It was a big, red, dusty book, with yellowing pages which crackled crisply as they were turned. On the front cover, in faded gold letters was written: *The Works of Samuel Taylor Coleridge.*

After a short while it became fantastically obvious to the two boys that the book was nothing less than a collection of the most magical of magic spells which they had ever had the good fortune to discover. There were

spells which made fair maidens fall in love with you, or changed old people into young children again, or brought summer back even in the middle of the coldest winter.

"Samuel Taylor Coleridge," sighed Sunday, "he must be a *very* powerful witch-doctor – we must tell no one about this," and they swore their most serious oath of silence, about eating dead frogs if you ever told.

"Good gracious!" said Johnbo', and "Tixo!" said Sunday, which meant more or less the same thing, for they had both seen a spell of the most fantastic proportions that quite took their breath away.

It was all about Kubla Khan, Johnbo's Grandfather's ostrich, who lived in a field on the top of the highest hill on the farm. In a flash Johnbo' remembered just how magical ostriches were, and how he had heard of one who could turn pink or purple or orange just whenever it wanted to, and could probably also make itself invisible. Sunday had once heard of some men, a long time ago, who had found a diamond the size of an elephant's eye in the stomach of an ostrich.

The spell was very wondrous, and a little scary. It was all about "incense-bearing trees" and "caverns measureless to man", which means that when you try to measure them you'll run out of tape-measure before you run out of cave.

The last bit of the spell, being obviously the most important, was read aloud by Johnbo', in his most mysterious voice:

"Weave a circle round him thrice
And close your eyes in holy dread.
For he on honey-dew hath fed
And drunk the milk of Paradise."

"There's a bottle of Honey-dew cooldrink in the cupboard downstairs," said Johnbo'. "It gives me hiccups when I drink it, but it sure tastes like paradise."

"So what we have to do is . . ."

"Get Kubla Khan to drink some Honey-dew cooldrink . . ."

"Then walk around him thrice times . . ."

"Three times, stupid!"

"Then close our eyes, and . . ."

"He'll get the hiccups and . . ."

"As sure as nuts he'll hiccup that diamond right out of his beak!"

Then "Good gracious," said Johnbo', and "Tixo," said Sunday, and their faces shone with the sheer pleasure of it all.

After much discussion, and the swearing of an oath doubly as powerful as the last one, the boys settled on the best date and time for the magic spell to be cast. The date was the 23rd day of April, which fortunately happened to be that particular day, so they wouldn't have to wait too long, and the time was midnight, because everyone knows that magic is ten times more powerful when it is cast by the light of the midnight moon.

The rest of that day was spent in an exhilarating haze of plans and excitement. Sunday and Johnbo' played "packed-sardines" with the other farm children, who would have been wildly jealous if they had even begun to suspect the amazing ostrich-and-diamond-and-incredible-riches-type thoughts whizzing around the two boys' heads.

When the boys were playing cards with Johnbo's mother after afternoon tea, Sunday said "ostrich" instead of "snap" and the boys collapsed in a heap of uncontrollable giggles. Mrs van Zyl hoped that they weren't sickening for something nasty like chicken-pox or influenza.

She got even more worried when Johnbo' said he thought he'd have an early night that night, something he had only done twice before in his life – once when he woke up the next morning with measles and once when he woke up the next morning covered in red paint.

At exactly ten minutes before midnight, Johnbo' crept quietly, toothbrush mug in hand, down the long flight of stairs to the entrance hall, stopping only to obtain two chocolate crisp cookies from the jar in the pantry. Such emergency precautions were very important, as he had often heard of brave adventurers being trapped in dark ostrich fields with no food, and therefore nearly starving to death.

As quiet as a mouse with tonsilitis, Johnbo' filled his mug with Honey-dew cooldrink, then nearly spilt it all when he heard footsteps outside creeping up to the front door. A low, moaning call, like a pigeon-kind-of-owl, came echoing through the keyhole – and Johnbo' realised it was only Sunday, because his owl-calls always sounded like pigeons and his pigeon-calls always sounded like owls.

In two winks of an elephant's eye the two boys were running up the stony pathway to the place where Kubla Khan slept quietly in the unsuspecting moonlight. The night wind whispered hushed secrets to the silver trees, the crickets made cricket-noises and the boys made boy-noises, like giggling and gasping and talking in low, serious voices about the very, very powerful spell they were about to cast.

"Weave a circle round him thrice
And close your eyes in holy dread
For he on honey-dew hath fed
And drunk the milk of paradise."

So after a quick snack of emergency rations, and a few very tiny sips of Honey-dew, the boys began to weave a large, rustling circle about the huge, grey mound of Kubla Khan. A moonshadow jumped at Johnbo', who nearly dropped his precious mug of Honey-dew from the shock, then recovered quickly and suggested sensibly that they drink a little more of it, to prevent any further spillage.

The second circle was a little smaller than the first, as the boys felt a lot braver than they had the first time. After the third, bravest, smallest circle of all, Kubla Khan stirred, then rose to his enormous feet, shaking his neck and hissing loudly. The boys decided it was time to retreat, and to close their eyes in "holy dread", which actually meant that they were allowed to feel a little frightened, so they did.

"Now, I reckon," began Sunday, "you must get that ostrich to drink that stuff!"

"Then you grab that diamond, and we run back to the farmhouse," concluded Johnbo', with an air of calm dignity – then ruined it all by giving a very loud, undignified hiccup.

And so the boys began their silentish approach of the ostrich, who had lain down again, and appeared for all the world to be sound asleep. On their hands and knees they crawled, with wide white eyes and pounding hearts.

The next few minutes were a confusion of screams and squawks and hisses, and other scared-boy and scared-ostrich noises.

Johnbo', after careful thought, decided to throw his whole toothbrush mug at Kubla Khan, who rose to his toes, and rushed headlong at them – then somebody hiccuped, and the boys decided, without any discussion, that it was time for the running home bit. Off they sped down the hill, as if all the blackest magicians in Africa were at their heels.

Now I know what you're thinking. You're thinking: "Whatever happened to the diamond?" Well, to tell you the truth, when Johnbo' and Sunday collapsed in breathless relief at their front gate, they didn't quite know either, but neither of them actually wanted to mention it.

Then Sunday, who, like Johnbo', only wears shoes for special occasions like casting spells, pulled off his tackies – and what should fall out of his left tackie but a small, round, shiny stone.

"Sunday," said Johnbo', "this is a *diamond*".

And Sunday nodded in silent agreement and wonder at the amazement of it all.

Then "Good gracious!" said Johnbo' and "Tixo!" said Sunday, and they both sped back to their beds and dreamt all night of the fame and fortune which lay before them.

DID YOU KNOW?

Kubla Khan was emperor of China over seven hundred years ago. The great traveller Marco Polo visited him and was so impressed by the splendour of his court and palace that he stayed there, serving Kubla Khan, for seventeen years. (His name is sometimes spelled Kublai, and he was a grandson of the famous Genghis Khan.)

Samuel Taylor Coleridge was an English poet whose best-known poems are the strange dreamlike "Kubla Khan" and the very long, magical "Rime of the Ancient Mariner".

Raie Rodwell

A visit to the docks

Gamat and Ebrahim ran down the hilly street in the Malay Quarter where they lived, high above the city of Cape Town. They were excited because they were going to the docks with their father. He worked on a trawler and was helping with repairs before it set out on its next trip.

Their mother stood on the stoep of their house holding their baby sister in her arms.

"We'll catch a big fresh fish for you, Ma," called out Gamat as he waved goodbye to her. "It won't be frozen and hard like the ones from the trawler."

"That'll be nice," said his mother. "I'll cook it for supper. Look out and don't fall into the water."

Gamat and Ebrahim stopped on a corner to wait for their father, as they were far ahead of him, and peeped into the shop there. They liked the smell that came from all the spices used for making curry.

"Good morning, Mr Allie," they said to the owner, who was standing at the door. He had a friendly wrinkled face, and he was wearing his kufiya, a white crocheted skull-cap that the men and boys wore when they went to pray in the mosque. But many of the old men wore it every day.

"You going somewhere?" asked Mr Allie, shuffling out into the warm sun.

"Yes," said Gamat, "we're going to the docks with our pa."

"Lucky boys! When I was young, that was always my favourite place to visit and see the ships that went all over the world. A wonderful place!"

When their father joined them, Gamat asked, "Pa, can we have some slangetjies – please?"

"But you boys just had breakfast. All right, a small packet each."

"Have a good time," said Mr Allie, as he handed them the little biscuits. "And here's a pasella each."

"Thanks, Mr Allie," said the boys, pleased with the red suckers that he gave to them. In the supermarkets they never got pasellas, only in the little old shops like Mr Allie's.

They walked along enjoying the crispy biscuits thin as match sticks and shaped like tiny snakes. They crackled between their teeth and burnt their tongues like the hot curry their ma made.

At last they were at the dock gates. It was fun walking through the docks to the Victoria Basin, where the trawler was moored among all the other fishing boats. They passed loaded goods trains outside the long warehouse sheds and Gamat and Ebrahim walked along the shiny railway lines from one shed to the next. There was little activity, because it was Sunday, and the boys enjoyed chasing each other between the rows of empty trucks.

"Hey, be careful, you two, and don't trip over things," called out their Pa.

"We're having fun," laughed Ebrahim as he ran up the ramp of a platform in front of a shed and then jumped down with a loud whoop. "It's nice here in the docks."

When they reached the boat, which was called *South-Easter*, and climbed on board,

their pa said, "You boys can look around while I go into the cabin to change into my overall. But keep out of trouble – I don't want any accidents."

"Let's go into the wheelhouse first," suggested Gamat.

They liked the glassed-in wheelhouse where the skipper stood and controlled the steering of the boat. Their father was second-in-charge and he also took his turn to steer. It was fine when the weather was good, their father told them, but when it was stormy and the boat rocked and plunged about in the waves as high as mountains, then it could be dangerous, especially if they were near the rocky coast.

There was a cap on a hook. Gamat put it on his head.

"Look," he laughed, "I'm the skipper." He held the wheel and called out, as he turned it from side to side, "putt-putt, putt-putt."

"Hey, hey, pasop for those rocks," shouted Ebrahim, joining in the game.

"You silly or something? Of course I can see the rocks. Putt-putt, putt-putt."

"Can I be the skipper now?" asked Ebrahim.

"All right – but you're only my helper, so you can't be at the wheel for long."

Ebrahim couldn't wear the cap because it was too big for him and almost covered his eyes. He stood at the wheel, moving it from side to side and trying to make noises like his big brother. Without the cap he didn't feel like a real skipper, and he soon lost interest in the game.

"Let's go and see what Pa is doing."

"Only after I've looked at all these dials and things," said Gamat.

"Well, be quick," said Ebrahim, and went outside to jump up and down the gangway leading to the wheelhouse.

Their father was painting some planks with tar to protect them against rotting. They stood and watched him for a while. Then Gamat asked, "Can we go down to the quay and look at the water, Pa?"

"Sure, but be careful."

Ebrahim sat on the edge of the quay with his legs dangling and Gamat sat on one of the bollards round which the *South-Easter*'s mooring lines were tied. It was nice to listen to the creaking noise that the lines made as the boat rocked from side to side in the water. They ate the suckers Mr Allie had given to them and then finished the slangetjies.

"Look!" called out Gamat as he pointed at a place where the sparkling water suddenly broke into bubbles and turned into circles that spread wider and wider across the Basin. "It's a fish!"

"It's eating the slangetjies," said Ebrahim, peering into the water. "I emptied the crumbs out of my packet into the water."

Gamat jumped off the bollard. "I've got a good idea. We can try to catch it for Ma – remember we promised her a fish. Let's ask Pa for something we can catch fish with."

Their father wasn't too pleased about having to stop his work, but he went into the cabin and tied a hook onto a long piece of gut. He put a piece of bait on the hook.

"Thanks, Pa. Now we're going to catch that fish for supper."

For a long time they sat on the quay with their line in the water, but no fish came. A movement across the Basin caught their attention.

"Look at that seal," said Gamat, and they watched as he stretched himself out on the steps below the quay to enjoy the sun on his shiny skin. Suddenly Gamat, who was holding the line, gave a whoop. "I can feel the fish at the bait. I'll wait till it's got the hook right in its mouth, then I'll pull it up."

"Wow, wow!" called out Ebrahim. "I hope it's a big one."

"I think it's a harder," said Gamat as he drew the fish slowly to the surface. It thrashed about, churning up the water.

What they didn't see in their excitement was that the fat old seal wasn't on the steps across the Basin, and that a shiny nose was coming nearer and nearer to them. Suddenly there was a tremendous tug on the line, and Gamat almost lost his balance. They could hardly believe what had happened, it had been so quick. The seal had stolen their fish and was swimming away with it in his mouth.

"You thief!" shouted Gamat as they watched the seal heave himself up the steps and then sit chewing the fish that was really theirs.

"Pa! Pa!" yelled Gamat, hopping up and down. "We caught a fish, and then that seal over there came and pinched it."

Their father leaned over the side of the boat and burst out laughing.

"Why are you laughing? It's not funny."

"Ag, that lazy old skelm," said their father, "don't be too cross with him. We know him well. He's Pop-eye the Sailor. Didn't you see that he has only one eye? He must have lost an eye in a fight. Those male seals are regular fighters when they're young. But now he's old and lazy. He lives in the Basin, and we always give him bits to eat."

Gamat and Ebrahim laughed with their father as they looked across at the sneaky old seal.

"Well," said their father, "you won't be having your fresh fish for supper, but old Pop-eye enjoyed it for lunch."

"But it would have been nice," said Gamat, "to take home a fish to Ma – one we'd caught ourselves."

DID YOU KNOW?

South Africa's coastline is nearly 3 000 kilometres long, but there are only nine true harbours. (The full list is: Port Nolloth, Saldanha Bay, Table Bay, Simonstown, Mossel Bay, Port Elizabeth, East London, Durban and Richards Bay.) Ships in *Table Bay harbour* in the early days of Jan van Riebeeck had no shelter from the north-west gales. Nine ships were wrecked and over two hundred people drowned during one storm in 1737. So they decided to build the first breakwater out into Table Bay to provide shelter for ships in winter. Every farmer bringing produce to the Cape Town market was ordered to use his cart and oxen to haul a load of stones to build the breakwater. The building was interrupted by a plague of locusts, for the farmers, having no crops to sell, did not come to town.

The first enclosed dock was ready for shipping in 1870. Many other docks have been built since, and the latest basin is called the Ben Schoeman Dock. Today, Table Bay harbour is used by fishing craft, yachts, oil tankers, passenger liners, and all sorts of cargo carriers.

Margaret Stodel

The dassie's dream

It was the end of summer and the earth was dry and parched. No rain had fallen for many months, and the mountain, with its many rocks and caves, waited patiently and silently for the cooler winds and clouds of autumn which might bring the rain.

In the caves lived families of dassies. The younger ones did not mind the heat and drought. Each day they played on the rocks, lay in the sun's warmth and told each other about their dreams. One had dreamt that he was a little tadpole and could swim in the pond and see everything under the water.

One little dassie was sad because he had never had a dream.

One day he decided to find out all about dreams. So when all the young dassies were playing on the rocks, he slipped away and hopped down the dusty mountain. He heard a slithering and hissing, and there before him was a long snake. The little dassie's mother had told him never to speak to strange snakes, but he had to ask him, "Snake, please can you tell me, do you have dreams?"

"Oh yes, I do, and sometimes I dream that I have a nice little dassie to eat for my supper."

The little dassie was frightened and ran away, down the mountain.

Next, he met a big old tortoise, creeping slowly up the steep mountainside. The tortoise pulled in his head and tail when he saw the dassie, for he was very shy.

"Tortoise, please tell me, do you have dreams?" asked the dassie.

"Ah, yes," said the tortoise, poking his head out of his shell, "I do. Would you like me to tell you of my best dreams?"

"Yes, please."

"Well, I often dream that I have come to the end of my journey, to a place green and cool with long grass and shady trees, and with a cool stream where I can bathe my aching feet, and drink when I want to." Suddenly the tortoise started walking off again, quite fast, as though he knew he would soon come to the end of his journey.

The little dassie went on sadly, and wondering whether he would ever meet

anyone who could help him find a dream. On a rock just ahead was a lizard sunning himself. The dassie nearly didn't see him, because he was the exact colour of the rock. When the dassie came closer the lizard lifted his head. They looked at each other. "Lizard, please tell me, do you have dreams?"

"Yes, beautiful dreams."

"Can I have one?"

"Of course. Do you see that cave over there? Go there and you will see something very special. If you sleep there you will have a very beautiful dream."

The little dassie ran to the cave.

At first he couldn't see anything at all, as the cave was so dark inside. But then he saw, on the rock that formed the back of the cave, beautiful paintings of animals. Elephants with large tusks, delicate little buck and some men with bows and arrows. He knew what they were even though he had never seen real elephants, or buck, or Bushmen before, because his father had told him about them. His father had been told by his grandfather and he by his grandfather and so the story had been passed on. The little dassie sat and gazed at the pictures. He was tired after running down the mountain. It was nice and cool inside the cave. He lay down and soon fell fast asleep. And then he had a dream of his very own.

He dreamt that he was sitting on a rock looking out over the valley. But the valley was not dry and sandy and barren as it was now. It was green and fertile, with lush grasses and bushes laden with red berries. The trees were full of ripe wild fruit, and animals and birds were everywhere. The river was not nearly dried out and full of rocks, but wide and deep and blue. Elephants were there, drinking and playing, buck were walking up and down at the edge of the water, and there were the Bushmen chattering to each other while they filled their leather bags with berries and leaves. Then he heard someone say, "Good afternoon, young fellow, welcome to our valley." He looked around and there was his great-great-great-great-grandfather. He knew at once who it was; he was very, very old, his fur was a beautiful silver grey with cloudy-white patches around his nose and mouth. His eyes were shining and clear and he looked very wise, as though he knew every secret in every heart.

Little Dassie was very happy. His great-great-great-great-grandfather said to him, "I am always here on this rock, and always will be. You can visit me any time you wish."

The dassie woke up, and still with great joy in his heart he ran home, thinking of his beautiful dream, and his great-great-great-great-grandfather waiting for him to visit him at any time. He also knew, with great certainty, that dreams are just waiting, somewhere, for anyone who searches long and hard enough.

DID YOU KNOW?

The nervous brown *dassie* is also called rock-rabbit and hyrax, and may even be the cony mentioned in the Bible. Dassies live in families, and come out in the early morning and late evening to feed on leaves and greenery with their strong teeth. They have four toes on their front feet and three on their back feet. Like you and me, they love basking in the sun, but their sharp eyes spot strangers very quickly and they make chattering and whistling calls to each other as alarm signals. So they have usually disappeared by the time we get there!

Dianne Stewart

The orange tree

It was a time of drought and sadness. The veld was becoming drier and drier, and the grass hard and brittle. The rivers and springs had dried up, and people had to walk further and further to find drinking water.

A little boy, Dumi, sat on the dusty ground outside his mud hut and watched the fowls pecking expectantly for food in the dry, barren earth. The mealies had died from lack of water and stood abandoned in the field in front of him. Next to the house stood an old withered tree, that was dying too from lack of moisture. He looked into the clear blue sky above him, but it held no hope of rain.

Suddenly tears flowed from his eyes and his sobbing was heard by his mother and his sister.

"Why are you crying?" asked Thembani, his sister.

"I am hungry and there is no food. I am thirsty and there is little water to drink," said Dumi.

"I am hungry and thirsty too," said Thembani.

The tears rolled down their faces, wetting their cheeks, and fell onto the iron-hard earth. These tears of sadness were quickly gobbled up by the dry, thirsty earth.

Sikazi, their mother, held them tightly in her arms and tried to comfort them. Little Dumi caught sight of the old gnarled tree that grew outside the house and said: "What kind of tree is that?"

"It is an orange tree," said Sikazi. "It once produced the sweetest oranges that I have ever tasted. But look at it now. It has almost died because of the drought."

A little while later, an idea came to life in Dumi's mind. He told his sister of his plan and together they left their home and walked across the veld. On Thembani's head she carried a silver billy-can which sparkled as it caught the rays of the morning sun.

After a very long walk along the dusty paths, the children arrived at a tiny trickle of water that had once been a running stream. Many people had gathered there to fill their containers with water. Dumi and Thembani carefully filled their billy-can, and then set off on the long journey home. They were happy and their song carried across the veld.

Thembani and Dumi were very tired and thirsty when they eventually arrived home. The cool, clear water from the billy-can quickly quenched their thirst. They transferred some to the large jug inside their hut that was used for storing all the water they could find, and then rushed outside with what remained. They carefully poured it onto the base of the gnarled old orange tree, where it was quickly taken by the dry, dry soil.

Each day Dumi and Thembani travelled a long distance to find a little water for their orange tree. A few months later, they noticed that the branches had given birth to a mass of bright green leaves. It seemed miraculous, in the midst of the drought.

Then white flowers that smelled as sweet as honey blossomed all over the tree.

"They are beautiful," said Sikazi.

When passing by, people often stopped to marvel at the lush, green tree. Bees buzzed around the blossoms gathering nectar, birds came to rest in its branches, and children found shade beneath it, away from the hot rays of the summer sun.

One morning, as Dumi and Thembani stepped outside their home, they noticed large, green fruit on the tree. They longed to pick it. The skin of the fruit felt rough in their hands.

"Wait until the fruit is ripe before you pick it," said Sikazi to the children.

Before long, the hot sun had ripened the fruit on the tree, turning it into bright yellow oranges. Thembani plucked an orange from the tree, and rolled it between the palms of her hands. As she plunged her thumb into the top of it, a fine spray rose in the air. She put the orange to her dry lips and sucked the juice. It quenched her thirst.

Dumi dug his nails into the fruit and peeled off chunks of the yellow skin. He removed the white pith from around the juicy segments and divided the orange into quarters. "Try some," he said, as he handed a piece to his mother.

"There is so much fruit on this tree," said Sikazi. "We must share it with our neighbours."

The children ran off to tell their neighbours and friends to come and fetch some oranges from their tree.

"They are so sweet," said the children to their friends.

Sikazi was generous and shared all the fruit that she had. It amazed her that the tree kept on bearing fruit. Dumi said that this was because he watered it every day, even though he had to walk a long distance to find the water.

All the people who had been given Sikazi's oranges saved the tiny pips that were inside each orange, and planted them near their homes. The little water they could spare was used to water the pips in the dry ground. The pips grew into baby orange trees.

All the time, children in every village were searching for water to feed their trees. Soon, orange trees were sprouting and flourishing all over the drought-stricken veld, next to the huts. The fruit was shared around with those who had none. The orange trees became known as the trees of happiness as they provided both food and moisture for the people.

One grumpy old woman, Dumela, watered her pips very well, and watched with delight as her tree bent over with the burden of lush, sun-ripened oranges.

"There are so many oranges on my tree, but I am too old and tired to take them to my neighbours. No one will mind if I keep them for myself," said Dumela.

She decided to pick them and store them in her house, so that she would have plenty of food during the long drought. She started picking at sunrise, and was still picking the fruit off her tree when the sun set.

"My back aches," said Dumela, "but now I have a good supply of oranges that no one knows about."

A few days later, she went outside to inspect her tree. To her horror, she discovered that it had shrivelled and died. The lush, green leaves had dried and turned brown, leaving what seemed only a dry brown skeleton tree. At the sight of this she felt ill, and returned inside to escape the hot, blazing sun. She lay down.

"I have a fever and my head throbs with pain," she cried.

Her moans and groans echoed across the veld and were heard by Dumi and Thembani. They were sitting in the shade of their orange tree.

They rushed over to Dumela's house and found her lying on the floor, complaining of a headache.

"Let us give her some sweet orange juice," said Thembani. She looked around the room, but could find no trace of an orange. Thembani rushed home in search of some oranges for Dumela.

She soon returned with a blue enamel mug filled with squeezed juice. As the old woman took a sip, she burst into tears.

"I have been so selfish," she cried. "I did not share my oranges with all the people who have none and are thirsty. Now my tree has died."

Tears poured down her wrinkled face. She drank the sweet liquid and slowly her health returned. Her fever subsided and her headache stopped.

"I promise that in future I shall share all the oranges I have," said Dumela.

She pointed to a cupboard which was filled with rotten oranges that had become over-ripe before she had had a chance to eat them. "You may go now, children," she said.

Quietly the two children left the old woman and planted the seeds from the squeezed oranges outside her home. Because she was sorry about what she had done, the children hoped that the pips would grow into two healthy, strong orange trees.

They did grow into two large trees. When Dumela was cooking or resting inside, the sweet aroma of orange blossoms wafted in through the doorway of her home. She kept a few oranges for herself, but gave generously to those in need.

Even though she could not travel long distances to share her fruit, she invited people from near and far to collect the oranges from her home. Her trees continued to bear fruit.

The orange tree had indeed become the tree of happiness.

Jay Heale

Two boys and a dimo

There was once, so they say, a boy who was just too sure of himself. He thought he knew all the answers, and he didn't listen to any advice.

This boy was called Masilo and he lived in a neat little house on a high hill. All the families in his village were proud of their herds of cattle and sheep and goats. Some families kept their boys at home to look after the cattle, but Masilo was one of the lucky ones. He was able to go to school.

Each day his mother would wake him early, fill his tummy with a good bowl of porridge, and dress him in his smart school clothes. Underpants, trousers, shirt, hat and smart new shoes – all of them new only three weeks ago from the big store in the town two valleys away.

So Masilo had been at school for all of three weeks, but already he thought he had learnt everything. What was the point of sitting on a hard bench beside his friend Thabo, studying from dull books or reading dull words on a blackboard? He could be out in the fresh air having adventures.

So, one morning, Masilo made up his mind. His mother had fed him and dressed him and kissed him goodbye. Masilo waved his hand and ran down the hill past the other huts and houses, but he was not going to school today. Oh no – he had decided to go out into the wide world by himself.

He hid until he saw the bus that took them off to school driving away in a cloud of dust, and then started off in the opposite direction. The road was empty, as all the other children were either tending the animals or working at school. So it was quite a while before Masilo met anyone, and it was a strange person he met. A tall, strong giant of a man who stepped out from the shadow beneath a thorn tree so suddenly that he seemed to come out of nowhere. He was wearing nothing but a strip of skin tied around his waist. If Masilo had had more sense, he might have been careful of such a stranger. But Masilo decided he wanted some company, so the two of them walked along together.

Now the strange man was actually a dimo, a giant who often disguised himself as an ordinary human being. If Masilo had listened more to the stories at home and at school, he might have known better. But Masilo thought he knew everything, and he never bothered to listen.

The day grew hotter as the sun climbed and there was no shade on that part of the dusty road.

"That is a fine hat," said the dimo. "Far too fine for a boy like you. Here am I with my head burning in the sun. Do you not know that it is bad manners for a boy to wear a hat while a grown man has none? Didn't they tell you that at school?"

Masilo had never heard of a custom like that, but he didn't want to admit that he wasn't as clever as he thought he was. So he gave the stranger his hat.

A little further on, the dimo said, "Have you no respect for your elders? Have you never heard the rule that men over fifty

years old must wear a shirt? Why should you want me to break the law? I'm sure you learnt all about that at school."

Here was something else which Masilo had never heard of. But once again he wasn't going to admit it. Oh no! It was far easier to give the man his new shirt. He had been without a shirt often before, thought Masilo, so what did it matter now?

Down the hill and up the next one, to a log under a marula tree. There the dimo sat down and said, "What sort of manners do you have? Is it right for a man like myself to walk along with his shirt-tails flapping in the wind? Take off your trousers and give them to me. That is the right thing for you to do. Haven't they taught you anything at school?"

So Masilo, who was beginning to feel the strange magic of the dimo take control of him, took off his fine grey pants and handed them over. He didn't stop to wonder how it was that his own boy's pants became large enough for this great stranger. He did feel a bit funny, though, walking along dressed only in his underpants and his shiny black shoes.

Round the corner and round another, to where the road dipped down towards the river. The rains had washed away the surface in many places, and the stones were loose and sharp.

"Have you never learnt that it is dangerous for grown men to trip and stumble on bad roads?" demanded the dimo. "Surely your schoolteacher told you that?"

Without even thinking, Masilo took off his new shoes and gave them to the dimo, who put them easily on his huge feet without even saying thank you.

Down the road they went and down to the river, where a few pools lay among the rocks. "You're very dusty," said the dimo. "I'm sure your school lessons taught you to wash at least three times a day."

So Masilo found himself dipping into the stinking green water with its floating weed, and coming out more dirty than he had been before, while the dimo grabbed his underpants from the rock where he had put them. They went on from there with the dimo fully dressed and Masilo following him naked and feeling really rather foolish.

That was how they were when they came to the next village. The day was coming to its end, and the villagers stopped to gaze at this well-dressed stranger and the dirty naked boy behind him. They welcomed the dimo to sleep in the best house in the village, but no one wanted Masilo.

The dimo waved his arm and said, "Don't ask me who this stupid child is. I found him on the road. He knows nothing and is worth nothing. Just give him a scrap of food in a dirty dish, and let him sleep in a dirty hut. But take care – he might eat your sheep."

Poor Masilo was glad even for the cracked and muddy hut to shelter in. He was tired and ashamed and fell asleep quickly.

Now it happened that Thabo, Masilo's school-friend, lived in this same village. The bus had dropped him off after school, he had walked down to the village, changed out of his school clothes, done his homework, and so it was late when he was told that the dimo had been invited to stay the night in his family's house and that a strange boy was sleeping in their old hut.

Thabo was not so stupid as Masilo. He didn't like the look of the dimo at all. There was a nasty glint in the dimo's eyes, thought Thabo, as he settled down to sleep after supper. And at midnight, when the dimo slipped quietly out of the house, Thabo quietly followed him.

First the dimo went to the kraal and caught a fine sheep. With his bare hands he twisted its neck, killed it and then sat down to eat it. As he did, he chuckled to himself, "I'll wipe the blood on that stupid boy and everyone will believe he killed the sheep."

Thabo overheard this. He went to the hut and recognised poor Masilo asleep. Now Thabo had learnt more from lessons at school and at home than Masilo, and he thought he knew how to deal with the dimo. Quickly he ran home and took the horns of medicine which hung on the wall. These had been prepared specially by the Tswana doctor in the village, and they held special powers. He ran back to the hut where Masilo was curled up, shivering and still asleep, and he buried the horns in a circle around the earth floor.

Thabo was only just in time. He had just covered over the last horn and darted back to hide in the deep shadow of the kraal wall when the dimo arrived with a leg of sheep all dripping with blood. Still chuckling, the huge dimo crept towards the sleeping boy, intending to smear the blood all over him. But as he entered the hut, the horns started crying –

"Who comes here?
A dimo comes.
What is he carrying?
Bones and blood."

The dimo stepped back, puzzled, and went away. Thabo could see him, standing out in the moonlight, scratching his hairy head. After a while he crept back into the hut, and once again the horns hidden in the floor started to sing –

"Who comes here?
A dimo comes.
What is he carrying?
Bones and blood."

The dimo didn't want to be caught with the blood still on his own hands. He paused and looked around. The village still seemed quiet. So, a third time, he went inside and took one step over the circle of the medicine horns.

Immediately they all sang out with ringing voices –

"Who comes here?
A dimo comes.
What is he carrying?
Bones and blood."

The whole village was awake. Men seized their clubs and ran to find out what was wrong. Even then the dimo might have escaped if Thabo hadn't opened the gate of the kraal. Out came the sheep and goats, frightened by all the noise, and they knocked the dimo over in the middle of the road and trampled all over him. There he lay with the sheep's leg still in his hand, so everyone knew who he was and what he had done. So they killed him, and burnt him in a fire made of white wood, till there were only bare bones left.

Jenny Seed

Inkonjane

All summer Inkonjane, the swallow, had been very happy, but now everything was beginning to change. It was no fun any more to swoop down out of the warm skies with the other swallows.

It was no fun any more to skim over the lake so that his long, narrow, pointed wings and his forked tail almost touched the water.

Even the mud nest under the eaves of the pretty cottage in Herefordshire in England did not seem as comfortable and as cosy as it had at the beginning.

For some weeks, ever since Inkonjane and his brothers and sisters had hatched out of the speckled eggs in the nest under the eaves, he had been trying to grow into a good swallow. He had been trying to do everything a swallow was meant to do. It was not always easy. Even his mother and father did not help him very much. He had to learn most things for himself.

He watched the big swallows swoop and glide with outspread wings, and he swooped and glided too. He saw how they caught insects for their dinner on the wing, and he caught insects in the same way. And he learnt to fold his wings and to fly straight down under the eaves into the nest as his mother and father did.

All these things he knew a swallow was meant to do.

He was very happy just being a swallow until in September it began to grow cold.

Inkonjane did not like the cold. It made him feel restless and cross and miserable. He fretted and fussed. Instead of flying joyfully out of the nest every morning as soon as it was light, he made excuses to stay behind in the warm straw and feathers.

His mother became impatient with him.

"Inkonjane!" she scolded one day when she saw that he was the last out of the nest again. "I am beginning to think that you are not a good swallow. All the other swallows are out in the sky already."

"I try to be a good swallow, Mother," chirped Inkonjane. "I really do. It's just . . . It's just . . ."

He did not want to tell his mother that it was the cold that kept him so long in the nest, so he said, "There is a question that worries me."

"What question, Inkonjane?"

"Why is my name Inkonjane, Mother?" he asked. "It is such an odd kind of name."

"It is your Zulu name," his mother replied. "That is what you are called in Zululand in Africa. Inkonjane means a swallow."

Inkonjane was very puzzled. "But where is Zululand, Mother?" he said. "We live in England. Where is Zululand?"

"Zululand is a country far far away."

Inkonjane was even more puzzled. "Then what has Zululand to do with me?" he asked.

His mother would listen no longer. "Inkonjane!" she said. "Stop asking questions. The sun is already high in the sky. You must go out to practise your flying."

Inkonjane ruffled his feathers unhappily and crept out of the mud nest.

"Now remember," his mother called after him, "practise well. Your wings must grow

strong because you will need them soon."

"Why?" chirped Inkonjane. "Why, Mother? Why?"

But his mother had already flown away and there was no one to tell him why he would need strong wings soon.

Inkonjane flew off too. He soared up into the crisp air. Then he swooped and glided as fast as he could. He caught insects on the wing. But nothing he did made him feel any happier.

"What is the matter, Inkonjane?" asked a large toad that was sitting on a stone between the tufts of water grass beside the lake. Inkonjane darted quickly over the stone. The black feathers on his back shone blue in the sun.

"I do not like the cold, Toad," he said miserably. "Do you feel the cold? What can I do to keep warm?"

The toad gave a loud croak and puffed up his neck. He stared up at Inkonjane with his golden speckled eyes. "The cold does not worry me," he said. " If you are cold you should do as I do. During winter I make a hollow in the ground under a nice smooth stone and go to sleep in it. You should try it." With that he plopped into the water and disappeared.

Inkonjane gazed at the wet ground and the cold moss-covered stones. They made him feel more miserable still. He had never heard of a swallow sleeping under a stone. He did not think that that was what a swallow was meant to do.

Off he flew again and came to rest on the telephone wires near a meadow where sheep were grazing.

"How can I keep warm?" he asked crossly.

An old woolly sheep looked up and blinked at him. "Do as I do," the sheep said. "Grow a thick woolly coat like mine. That will keep you warm in the cold weather."

Inkonjane cocked his head. He glanced down at the rusty red feathers on his breast. He turned and examined his smart blue-black tail feathers. He had never heard of a swallow growing wool. He did not think that that was how a swallow was meant to keep warm.

Then one day about a week later he saw a crowd of swallows sitting side by side on the telephone wires along the road next to the cottage. Every now and then some would fly off, then swoop back to take their place again with the others. They all seemed excited, as if something important were going to happen. Inkonjane's mother and father were there too.

"What is happening?" he asked as he came to sit beside them. He too all at once was beginning to feel excited. He had never seen the swallows gathered like this before.

But his mother was far too busy chirping to her neighbour to take any notice of Inkonjane. His father only said, "How many times must we tell you not to ask so many questions?"

Inkonjane the swallow would have to find out for himself.

After a while the swallows all flew away and the telephone wires were left empty. The next day the swallows came together again. And the day after that. And the day after that. Every day the excitement grew.

Inkonjane gathered with the other swallows. He sat impatiently on the wires, waiting. Then suddenly one day his mother turned to him and said, "I hope you have been practising your flying like a good little swallow."

"Yes, Mother," said Inkonjane. "I can fly very far now without getting tired. I can fly almost as well as you and Father now."

"I am glad to hear that, Inkonjane," said his mother. "Do you see what a good swallow he is?" she said to her neighbour.

Then she turned back to Inkonjane. "Come on, then. Are you ready?"

"Ready for what?" asked Inkonjane, almost bursting with curiosity.

"Ready to go to Zululand, of course," said his father.

"Zululand!" So Zululand did have something to do with him after all.

"I told you about Zululand," said his mother. "You have a Zulu name – Inkonjane. When it is winter here in England we go to Zululand in the south where it is summer and it is warm. We have a very comfortable nest under the grass roof of a mud house in Zululand. I told you that you would need strong wings. We have a long, long way to fly."

With that his mother and his father, his brothers and his sisters and all the swallows on the telephone wires rose up into the sky.

They swooped across the lake, twittering and whistling and calling to each other. They darted over the pretty cottage in Herefordshire which had been Inkonjane's home. Then they all flew away in a great crowd towards the south.

Inkonjane went with them. He was no longer restless. He was no longer miserable. He was no longer even cold. He raced through the chilly air as fast as he could. And he was happy because he knew that he was going to the warm south for the winter. He knew at last that that was what a swallow was meant to do.

For many days the swallows flew southward, over mountains and over seas and over deserts.

At last below them Inkonjane could see a lovely land with sunny hills and grassy slopes. On a hill was a group of mud houses with grass roofs.

"Come, Inkonjane," said his mother. "This is Zululand, and there is the Zulu house where we are going to live."

Inkonjane looked down in excitement. In front of one of the houses a small black Zulu boy was standing gazing up at the birds.

"Look, my father!" the boy called out. "Summertime is coming. The swallows have returned. Inkonjane is here."

DID YOU KNOW?

Migration is a long word we use to mean the way that some types of bird move from one country to another, keeping with the warm weather. Some (like the sandpiper and the Arctic tern) make a journey of over ten thousand kilometres every year. Bird-watchers sometimes catch some of these migratory birds and put a tiny ring on one leg. Swallows from South Africa have been seen again in England, in Germany, even as far north as Russia. Most of the European swallows arrive here around November, and leave in March or April.

Other birds that migrate to South Africa include the "piet-my-vrou", the stork and the garden warbler.

Christopher Gregorowski

The first Sunflower

There was a time, you know, when there weren't any Sunflowers at all, but only Groundflowers.

In those days they had long green stems and brown faces, but that was all. No golden-yellow petals. And they didn't look at the sun each day. Oh no, they looked at the earth, stooping over and watching the ground all day. That's why they had faces the colour of rich brown earth. And that's why they were called *Ground*flowers.

The Groundflowers were very contented with their lot, happy to stare at the ground which gave them food and drink and a home for their roots.

But there was one Groundflower who had been born alongside a small, quiet stream, and early one morning, on a lovely day, he caught sight of something so beautiful that he could hardly believe it. There, in the water, was a beautiful, shining, golden-yellow ball. Of course he didn't know that he was looking at a reflection of the rising sun. He couldn't take his eyes off it. Very soon it disappeared. He was very sad, and a teardrop fell into the ground at his feet.

But the next day, and the next and the next, the Groundflower saw his golden ball of light again. He learnt that by leaning out over the water, he could see it for a longer time, and when he leaned really dangerously far, he saw his own face in the water with the golden light surrounding it. This was a glorious vision, and he longed for it to be real. But of course it passed away, it vanished as visions do, and he spent the rest of

the next day and night just staring at the ground, waiting.

At night the Groundflowers used to share their news and views in whispers, as Sunflowers do now. Some had noticed the strange behaviour of the Groundflower by the river, and were more than a little displeased. A youngster should be taught to know his place and his station in life! But the Groundflower by the river took no heed. While the rest whispered their criticisms at night he longed for the dawn and the vision. On grey cloudy mornings he was restless and impatient.

It was about now that a little wind which passed by every day took pity on our friend. It was a small wind but a strong one. Just as the Groundflower leaned out over the river, dangerously (for roots can loosen, especially in the soft riverside), for a last glimpse of the glorious vision, the little wind pushed at his face again and again, lifting it skywards. It took many days of persistence on the wind's part, in the face of much opposition from the Groundflower, who complained about the awful pain in his neck.

It was only with the help of the Sunbird, with her long beak for honey-sucking, that the wind's purpose was accomplished. The Sunbird is a messenger from the Sun, just as the Rainbow is. On her back and neck and chest, her wings and tail, she displays every colour of the Sun's light. She didn't speak, but her actions spoke louder than words. She pecked at the Groundflower's face, not for the seeds, but to get him to straighten his neck and lift his face to the Sun.

Together they did it, the wind and the Sunbird. Our friend the Groundflower, pushed by the one and pulled by the other, saw with his own eyes, in one fleeting moment, the source of his vision, the Sun himself. From then onwards, helped by the little wind, he lifted his aching neck for longer and longer periods, to watch the Sun. The Sunbird no longer pecked at his face, but flew into his downward gaze, hovered, and swiftly flew upwards, again and again, giving encouragement with every wingbeat, reminding him of the Sun as the myriad of colours glinted in her feathers.

Now a strange thing had begun to happen to the Groundflower. The wind and the Sunbird had noticed this some time ago. It was this which had attracted their attention to him. A soft golden-yellow halo had appeared around his dark brown face. In fact, a definite fringe of petals was growing there. He was beginning to look like a picture of the Sun.

Of course the rest of the Groundflowers were furious. They were jealous and angry. They hissed their accusations at night, saying that he was endangering all the Groundflowers in the world. But the little wind was there, even at night, and the Sunbird in the morning, to give him strength. He went on looking at the Sun for longer and longer periods each day, for as long as his aching neck could stand it, until he was following the Sun from dawn to sunset as Sunflowers do today. And as he did so, his golden-yellow petals grew to magnificent proportions. He taught a few others to see the Vision in the quiet stream, and eventually, helped by the wind and the Sunbird, to lift their eyes to the Sun himself.

The time came for the Groundflowers to die, and leave their seed to grow up in the ground next year. Our friend died too, and so did his friends. They shed their seed, and they themselves were welcomed into the blazing heart of the Sun.

The seed they shed? It was not ordinary Groundflower seed. It was the seed of the Sunflower, and from it the next year grew a new family of Sunflowers who helped more Groundflowers to become true creatures of the Sun. And so they are to this day.